EVERY OPEN EYE

Our Shadows Will Remain

Book Three

ALEC CHARLES

Oxford eBooks

In this series:

Big City Secrets
Days of Surrender
Every Open Eye

1

I'VE BEEN STAYING at The Missionaries of Charity building in Tryfords for just over a week and I still have no idea whether the women in penguin getups are sisters or nuns. They insist on being called by their homely names like Sophia and Nicola but they don't want to give away their title so I don't give away mine. I let them call me Lee or Doyle depending on what age bracket they fall into. And sometimes I wonder if they're trying to catch me out. When I was first talking with Abigail- the one I figure is the head honcho- I noticed a picture of a middle aged Father or even Reverend in a framed picture and she told me that it was Antony but she didn't take the time to tell me whether it was Father Antony or Reverend Antony. She spoke so fast I couldn't be sure whether she had said he was out of the state to visit his own mother or a church mother. I don't know... Maybe she's hoping to catch me out, maybe my head is a little off from the kicking I got. I'd ask for a second opinion but a doctor at the nearest hospital might have one too many questions about my life so I put up with the pain at my sides whenever I get up to move. The swelling around my eyes is fading fast and that's good enough for me. If Doyle was still around, he'd be able to tell me for sure whether the first broken nose is always the worst and once that's out the way it's pretty much easy sailing.

But the building is pretty big. Bums come for a bed when it's getting dark and leave early morning but I haven't been given a time limit. Haven't been asked to contribute, haven't been pressed for my story until now because I've acted like something terrible has happened and they tend to back away for fear of causing me to break down in front of them.

And there's a girl, because there is always a girl. At a guess I'd say she's a little younger than me and she's cute as sin. Dirt-blonde hair with traces of fading green that must have been blue once. She looks to be staying here indefinitely because I've caught glances of her walking into closed rooms and talking to the other women but you just know she isn't church material. She smokes, too. I've seen her sat on the bench in the back a couple of times but she's always gone by the time I get out there and I tend to head back inside over staying with a life-size statue of Christ for company.

I have my own cigarettes. It took a few days but one of the penguins returned them to me on the promise that I only smoke them out back but I haven't smoked that many yet because every time I head out, the babe's vanished.

"Lee," Abigail says to me from the other side of what has to be Father or Reverend Antony's desk, "we want to help you but we can't help you as best as we can without the details. I'd thought you were quiet," she says, "from shock over the accident. I'd thought you were reflecting, taking a journey of self-exploration, but I believe there is more than that. Lee," she sighs, "we are here to help you. Will you help us in return?"

She says it all like a b-movie extra. If she isn't fully onto me, a part of her is. A part she would want to ignore because of the collar at my throat... The collar somebody here gave me. Doyle's is in my room, buried under the clean but previously loved shirts they've given me.

If Doyle was with me it'd be so much easier because he'd know what to say and I'd follow his lead. But Doyle isn't here. He left me but he didn't have a choice in the matter so you can't hold it against him.

I open my mouth and take in a little air- try to convince my body it's cigarette smoke that I'm bringing into it before putting the old vocal chords to good use.

"I'm thankful for your understanding," I start, "and the patience you've shown in my reluctance to share. But I'm ashamed," I say, "I'm ashamed my telling you what I've done will make you think less of me."

She makes a tight, barely noticeable smile of encouragement and reaches over the desk- placing a hand atop of mine. If the desk had been a decent size, she wouldn't have been able to do that. Her hand's cold but I can't move my own out from under it without losing the trust I'm out to steal from her. I try not to think about how those hands might never have touched a boner before- unless maybe she joined the church at a later stage in life. For all I know she came into it like I did. Stumbling in through a door and staying because nobody pressed her too hard for the truth.

"This is all so hard," I tell her.

"Go on," she says to encourage me. I bow my head and rub at closed eyelids like I'm trying to be rid of tears when really I'm encouraging them. The swelling's going down but they're still pretty sensitive.

"There was a woman," I say, looking up to her from under my eyebrows.

Abigail makes the smile again and nods. "What was her name?"

"Sophie," I tell her. "We started getting too close. It just felt so good," I say with a smile, "being around each other. I think people we're starting to wonder but I didn't care when she was around because I felt a joy in my heart like I hadn't for so long. Her husband, Howard, he's inside for a number of drugs offences and then some for good measure... So we became friends- me and Sophie, I mean. Offered one another comfort from hardship. People noticed and started talking... People who had always wanted to see nothing but good in me started seeing me in a new light and I can't say I blame them. Nothing had happened but I'm sure we both wanted it to.

"So I left," I say, rubbing at my eyes again. "Cleared a little time to free my head and got the first train out of there. I need to find myself but all I've found so far," I smile, "is a quiet stretch of road where the drivers drive fast and don't look back to see what they've hit."

Abigail gives that smile again and gives my hand another squeeze.

"I don't think you have done anything wrong," she says, "and I can't find fault with the plan of action you put in place. Tell me," she asks, leaning back in her chair, "do you have far to go before you're in the company of family or friends?"

Bitch looks to want me gone in a hurry.

"No," I say with a shamed smile, "I can't burden them with this... It just wouldn't be right. I'd rather stay someplace out of sight... Have people view me for the good I do and not the wrongs on my mind."

"I understand entirely. But you will have to go back home and face them," she says, "sooner or later."

"Then later," I smile, "when mind and body have had the time to recover."

She smiles at me but I know it isn't worth shit. She wants me out of here now and there's no denying it.

"I got to ask- do you know where my wallet is?"

"Your wallet?"

"Yes," I lie, "I remember having it in my pocket before the accident. Did you maybe put it someplace safe or could it still be out on the road where you found me?"

"I can't say I know," she says, getting to her feet to bring this meeting to an end, "but I can try and find out for you."

"That would be good of you," I smile, exaggerating the pain at my ribs while getting up. "If my staying here is going to be any trouble," I claim, "you simply have to say. I'll try and make a few calls- see if anybody would be kind enough to send any money my way."

"There's really no need," she smiles- passing me by to open the door for me, "you are more than welcome to stay here for as long as needed- or at least until Antony has returned and offered you his guidance. I simply have one rule for you to follow."

"No smoking indoors?"

"No," she smirks, "you lend a hand as soon as you are ready. As you may have noticed already," she continues, "we offer the unfortunate a place to stay for the night. We don't just provide a clean room and access to a warm meal but a shoulder to lean on and an ear to listen."

"I'd be proud to help you in any way I can for all you have given me."

She offers me a display of gratitude she doesn't honestly mean and watches me walk away from her little office with the eyes of a hawk, only closing the door behind her when I turn back to look at her. "Fuck this," I say with a sigh. There has to be somewhere nearby for me to score.

2

Walt's Drugstore.

I walk into the place with high hopes because it's only the sign that really stops the place from looking like a shotgun shack but my good mood falls to the dirty floor as soon as I spot the glass running the entire length of the counter. Everything of interest to me is kept from my touch. To get behind the counter you need to know the four digit code to open another door. A much stronger door than the one you first walk through... Most definitely reinforced. You wonder just what kind of regular Walt must have to deal with to feel the need for security measures like this. Getting around prison was easier.

"Can I help you, son?" an old man- Walt, clearly – asks, walking out from another door. I see a cramped room with tiled walls at his back, a toilet that must only cost a dollar or so more than an old paint tin. He keeps his eyes on me, pushes a hand back to close the door shut behind him and takes his time spotting the collar at my throat. "Forgive me," he smiles, "my mistake. I didn't see the collar," he explains.

"That's quite fine," I smile, watching him as he takes his time reaching the door that grants a man access to the real items of interest. He doesn't even glance back to make sure I can't eye him punching in the code. One finger slowly moves from one number to the next, pushing each one a lot harder and longer than necessary.

0... 3... 0... 1...

"This is a nice place," I offer with a smile, watching him take slow steps towards a stool positioned behind the cash register. "I didn't think small businesses like this were still running."

A cheap lie used as a compliment to try and earn the man's trust. You have to wonder, in a town like this, does he leave the doors unlocked at night because he figures a keycode and reinforced plastic is enough?

"Ha," he says, lowering himself down, "*towns* like this aren't really running, let alone independent stores like mine! How long have you been in Tryfords?" he asks.

"A week," I tell him, "give or take."

My eyes are on him but I'm still taking in everything on display, everything that isn't bolted into place or kept within touching distance, and it's a chore not to hide my disappointment.

Cheap sanitary towels you couldn't depend on to clear-up spilled coffee.

Bottles of aftershave with a bridge on the bottle.

"It's not much," he laughs, "is it? It's not much at all!"

A rotating display of cheap paperback books.

Greetings cards.

Comic books that were the latest issue half a year gone.

"Tryfords was a fine place back in the day," he claims.

Bars of soap with brand names from another era.

"They used to say every road here led the way to opportunity," he grins. "Have you *seen* the roads now? A car can't move twelve inches without finding a hole! Dead leaves and garbage left to rot in the drains," he continues, "and all they really lead to now are stores going out of business or underfunded services. This town was deliberately left to go *beyond* breaking point," he says, "and now they can't justify bringing it back.

"When I was a boy," he continues as the skin around his throat gets redder and redder, "my dad didn't believe in politics... Said one will rob you just as bad as another. So you know what he did? Used to ask me who I'd vote for and then he'd go vote for whoever I said. Never asked me why- just went and did it. Thought it was funny, probably. When it got to my time to cast a vote, I was more serious than he had ever been. I wanted to do what was best for my country so I voted Republican... Thought I always would," he says, "but never again. George W. gone did that," he says- somehow continuing without noticeably stopping for air, "gone made some bad calls and ruined his family name because of it. What he *intentionally* had happen to towns like this-"

"Mr Doyle?" someone says from right behind me. Having not

heard anybody else enter, I turn around in surprise to see who it is. Walt, who must have seen them coming in, somehow appears just as surprised. Maybe he's a man people rarely interrupt.

It's one of the penguins- Nicola, I think. Fresh faced, elfish hair and eyes that seem to hint at an inner cruelty longing to display itself. The way her mouth twitches, almost making at a smile, implies stopping old Walt mid-flow will have to do for now.

"I thought it was you," she says. "What are you doing here? Is anything the matter?"

"No," I tell her, "no- nothing's wrong... I just thought it time to meet some of the locals."

"I was just telling him," Walt says, "how Washington hasn't gave a damn about us for the last near-twenty years and it's down to people like you to pick up the pieces."

"We do what anybody else would do," she says to him with a smile, fingers taking my elbow to lead me away from here as best she can. "I'm sorry to drag Mr Doyle away from you like this," she claims, coaxing me back towards the door, "but I could use some assistance right now."

"Think nothing of it," Walt says with a wave of his hand. "Don't let it be said I wouldn't help out any more if I could."

We head back out onto the street and she keeps her fingers on my arm for a while and I can't help but picture us walking everywhere like this, looking quite the attractive couple. It's enough to make me reach for my cigarettes because I'm a firm believer that smoking makes a man look more appealing to the opposite sex.

"I'm sorry about that," she grins while I'm lighting a smoke, "but Walter is a man people have trouble getting away from once he gets going. I hope he didn't say anything too *blue*?"

"Nothing I haven't heard put better before," I shrug. "Is all that security back there necessary?" I ask her.

"No," she says. "Not too long after the Missionaries opened their doors, he had all of that added. He said we'd only attract more desperate people into town and they'd be robbing him blind."

"So what he was saying back then... About supporting your work?"

"Lip-service," she smiles. "He's a man of God and he thinks people like us will tell Him all the bad things he's been spouting. Whatever you do," she advises, "never tell him you think we need stricter gun control."

"You made that mistake before, huh?"

"No," she smirks, "but I've heard about the people who did and if I were one of them, I'd stay clear of the woods during hunting season."

3

TRYFORDS IS IN such a poor state, even Starbucks hasn't bothered to reach a tentacle in. It's Pete's Coffee House we go to because Tryfords is that kind of place. Pete's Coffee, Walt's Drugs, Jim's Garage, etc etc.

Nicola asks me, "What would you like?"

"What're you having?"

"A latte," she says.

"I'll have one of those."

"No problem," she says, "take a seat."

I grab an empty seat at an empty table. The tables- each and every one of them- are so small they'd struggle to hold a third cup of coffee. I doubt you could even rest a newspaper on one of them. Maybe that's why no one looks to have left one behind.

Nicola has a cheerful but brief conversation with the lone waitress before coming over with two lattes and a sugar dispenser on a plastic tray. "Here we are," she says.

"Thanks," I tell her. I consider making a joke about sugar dispensers having to be kept behind the counter because of thieving townsfolk but decide against it. "You come here a lot?" I ask, pouring sugar into my drink- hoping she'll notice just how much I'm taking and ask me about it.

"At least twice a week," she says, "more if I bump into somebody I know. It's a nice place. I think it has a nice smell."

"Fresh coffee and table wax."

"You've got it in one," she laughs. "Are you going for the record of most sugar in one cup?"

"Old habit," I smile. "Five sugars."

"Five?" she laughs. "It's a wonder you have any teeth left! How did that start?"

"Trying to be like my father," I tell her. "He was a good man."

"How long ago did you lose him? I'm sorry," she adds, "it's just I lost my own a little under two years ago now."

"He died earlier this year. Health related problems," I tell her with a smile, "not sugar related."

"How are you dealing with it?" she asks me with a caring smile of her own.

"I'm getting there... It's been hard and my head has been a little bit here and there at times, but I'm ready to see the world for how it really is again."

"That's good to know," she says. "I was the same- when my dad died. Even when you can see it coming, nothing can prepare you for it."

"Amen to that," I sigh. "What did he die of," I ask, "if you don't mind telling?"

"Lots of things," she sighs. "He was one of those people who just get one thing after another when they're getting older."

"Yeah," I say, "I know what you mean. Always thought it funny we wouldn't let an animal suffer the way we do our fellow man. But how about we change the subject to something a little lighter- or at least something with a lighter shade to it at the very least?"

"Okay," she grins. "How are you enjoying your stay in Tryfords?"

"It's quiet," I tell her, "feels like the set of a TV show being forgotten about. You don't have to go far to spot a place of business with boards on the window or a home with a sign outside letting you know the bank is now the owner."

Nicola nods, blows on her drink to cool it a little before taking a sip. "Before we arrived here," she says, "there was next to nowhere for people to get a little comfort. As sour and as sore as Walt can be, you can't help but understand him a little. This is one of many towns left to rot."

I nod as if in understanding. "How long have the Missionaries been here?" I ask her.

"Around ten years," she replies, "maybe more. We've been in the latest building the last five or six. The other place we had couldn't cope with the demand."

"So what do you do- travel around from town to town?"

"We're a charitable, non-profit organisation with our

headquarters in Seattle," she explains, "and there has been a large increase in the number of towns we reside in since the financial crash."

"I see," I tell her when I'm blinder than ever. I have no idea whether they're tied with any church in particular; whether they're really of the cloth of just people donning the colours. It's just a part of me *knows* I shouldn't grill her too much. Her little bunch could be something every *real* preacher worth his salt knows about. "So have you been here since the beginning?"

"No," she says, "three years. I was in Detroit before that. How's your latte?" she asks with a smile, watching me try it.

"Tastes like milky coffee," I answer and it makes her smile a little. "Any major differences between here and Detroit?"

She bows her head to drink a little more coffee, moving her body instead of the cup, and looks up at me from under her eyebrows to answer. Her eyes are a dark shade of brown. The irises look like they could be made of glass. I notice again how they make me think she could have a mean streak inside of her. "It's a lot smaller," she says.

"You know something- there's one thing I've been meaning to ask. You have a lot of rooms going spare, right? All those rooms and people turn up at night and leave early in the morning. Everybody but you," I say, "which is understandable, and myself- and the understanding is I won't be staying too long but while I am, I'll be working. So what's the girl's story?"

"Who?"

"The blonde. Looks like she used to colour her hair."

"Oh," she smiles, "you're talking about Elizabeth. She's helping us out but she's also paying for her room. We don't usually work like that," she says, "but Elizabeth is an unusual case."

"What makes you say that?"

"I can't really gossip," she tells me, "but you're free to ask her for her story."

"I would," I tell her, "but I rarely see her."

"She's working the soup kitchen tonight," she tells me, "you can ask her all about it if you go there."

"Maybe I will. You working there tonight?"

"No," she says with a shake of her head, "I have a lot of donated clothes to sift through."

4

ELIZABETH COMES HEADING out for a cigarette just as I'm lowering myself down on the bench near the statue of Christ and I wonder just what the fucking chances are- her coming out here like this after I'd been talking about her under an hour earlier. She sort of pauses on seeing me, smiles and keeps walking in my direction. I move along the bench a little even though there's no real need to. You could easily sit three, maybe even four people here.

"Thank you," she says, already lighting her cigarette whereas I'm still easing one from the pack.

"No problem," I reply; I light my cigarette and blow a little smoke to the breeze. Elizabeth takes another drag on her cigarette, looks up to the sky for a moment and then down to her feet. She taps one foot against the floor three, four times. "I'm Lee," I tell her.

"Nice to meet you," she says, facing me with a smile. Her eyes are beautiful; a delicate blend of pale blue and sparkling silver. Something about her reminds me of the girl I'd made plans with back in McFarlanes.

"Your name's Elizabeth, isn't it?"

She nods. "Most people call me Liz," she says, "or Beth."

"which do you prefer?"

"I'm easy," she laughs and it all falls silent again and I hope it doesn't last too long- that she'll rush her cigarette and walk away from me just as quickly. "You turned up a couple of days ago, didn't you?" She says, "Abigail was in a real panic because someone just turned up with you in the backseat of their car instead of rushing you over to the nearest hospital."

"I don't remember that."

"I suppose you wouldn't. But how are you doing? You holding up okay?"

"Sure," I nod. "It can hurt a little if I bend or move funny but that's about it. And the broken nose," I add with a shrug, "is nothing at all. It's a little tender around the eyes but they'll be fine soon enough."

"That's good to hear," she says, dragging a little smoke into her lungs before flicking dead ash to the ground. The breeze spreads it in no time at all. "Are you going to report it to the cops?"

"No," I say.

"You should," she says. "You might be recovering just fine but the next person mightn't be so lucky."

"Some driver probably took his eyes off the road for a second and didn't realise he'd hit a man," I sigh. "It was a dark night."

"You're very understanding."

"It's my job."

"I thought it was forgiveness?" she laughs.

"One hand washes the other," I shrug. "But what about you," I ask, "how did you end up here? This town," I tell her, "I don't think this is the kind of place where a girl like you would be born."

"Actually," she laughs, "I grew up in a town not too different from this one."

"So what happened? You taking a year out from studying?"

"A year out from life," she says. One sentence has me convinced she's no stranger to a shrink's office. Fairly recent, too. She says it like it's still new to her.

"Problems?"

"No one is to blame but myself," she says, taking a drag on her cigarette as she looks off into the distance. She's wondering how best to say whatever is on her mind. It's the collar at my throat, always encouraging people to go on.

"I find that a little hard to believe," I coax her. "Too many people take all the blame and you know something? I wish they wouldn't. I wish they'd look at the area they grew up in- the family they were saddled with and the politicians in place during their early years- and realise they were given the hand they were dealt by a cheat. Don't let anybody ever make you feel bad about yourself just because they don't want you blaming the assholes that pay their salary. A quick fix," I tell her, "doesn't work. They just want you to blame yourself so you get depressed and then hand more money over for drugs they own stock in.”

She looks at me a while and smiles. “You don’t talk like a priest,” she says.

“Because I’m not,” I smile. “Anyway,” I say, getting to my feet, “it was nice to finally get a chance to talk with you but I’d best start getting ready... I’m working the soup kitchen tonight.”

“Really?” She says in surprise, “So am I.”

“That’s good,” I smile, “I guess I’ll see you later. But before I go,” I jokingly add, “you’ve got to help me out here - do I call you Liz or Beth?”

“Liz,” she smiles.

“Liz,” I repeat back to her. “I look forward to working with you.”

5

I'M STANDING OUT front, smoking a cigarette and trying to find an easy way to get even a little money when a white van pulls up outside with a red Ford right behind it. The van driver hops out, slams the door and heads in my direction with a clipboard to hand. "I've brought the van," he says.

"I can see that."

He gives a look of mild bewilderment and takes a second or so to choose his words. "I've got *here* down for renting the van tonight."

The door to my back opens and one of the nuns or sisters or whatever else they might be quickly steps out in front of me. "Hello," she says to the driver, "where do I sign?"

He looks at me like he's not sure whether I was trying to fool him or not before handing the clipboard and attached document over to the woman of God. Sophia, I think. "Just in the third rectangle," he says. Sophia signs her name. The driver takes the clipboard back, says something like "God bless" to her and gives me one final quizzical look before making his way to the Ford that had parked up behind him. Once he's in the passenger seat, the vehicle moves away with him most likely telling the driver how I'm an asshole.

"Sorry about that," Sophia says to me, "you wouldn't have known about the van."

"You driving out to the beach?" I joke.

"It's for taking some things over to the kitchen," she says. "I'll just let Elizabeth know it's here," she adds, making her way back inside.

"Is it almost time for her to make tracks?"

"Yes," Sophia nods. There's a look in her eyes that says she's wondering just *what* it is to me exactly.

"Tell her to hold on for me a second," I say, tossing my cigarette out into the road, "and I'll be ready in no time at all."

6

The one bathroom I share with the penguins, the one bathroom we have that even the bums are permitted to use of a morning, has never bothered me before but it does now. I put it down to nerves because I'm getting ready to go out with Liz but I keep thinking of all the bacteria that must be there and I'll wash the soles of my feet because of it but then have to wash my hands again. In the end I give up, admit I'm as clean as I'm going to get and dry myself off with a towel before returning to my room with the towel around my waist.

It isn't a good towel. It's too rough, like drying yourself with sandpaper. Maybe they get towels like this so you can convince yourself you're scraping invisible dirt from your body.

The nerves follow me into my room. Trying to find the best clothes to change into and I can't help but think about how most of the clothes I have now were donated to the Missionaries. Dead-man's clothes. Even the spare collar they gave me could have been plucked from a cold throat and I should know because I've done that myself.

I want a cigarette. I want to use a deodorant that doesn't come in a pink can but know I can't afford to buy my own right now and Abigail will probably go on seeing I only get deodorant meant for women in her bid to get rid of me.

"Liz had best be worth it," I mutter under my breath.

I can't even ask her if she would like to go for a coffee once we're done at the kitchen because of how little money I have left. Will she think I'm a modern man if she invites me for coffee and I allow her to buy it- like I did Nicola? I've long thought women must go on about being our equals but hope for us to hold the doors open and buy their drinks.

I do what I can with my hair and check my reflection as best I can in the glass of a framed picture on the wall. I'm probably worrying about nothing when you consider how all the other men she'll see tonight must look.

I'll be fine as long as she sees me with a cigarette at least once.

7

It's still pretty light when we make our way to the van. I turn back to see if any of the others are watching us but don't see anyone. Maybe they have more important things to do, maybe they don't think anything will happen between us... Maybe it won't, but you'd have thought they would be excited to see me making a fool of myself.

"Do you rent the same van every time?" I ask as we clamber inside. It's been cleaned good and proper. The scented pine tree hanging from the mirror is probably fresh out of the seal.

"Same company," Liz says, bringing her seat closer to the wheel, "they give the Missionaries a discount."

"None of them drive?"

"One or two," she says, sliding the key into the ignition, "but I like to keep busy. I like to feel I'm doing good *and* earning my keep."

"I thought you paid for your room?" I ask as the engine comes to life.

"I do," she nods, turning the mirror a notch, "but it's not like I could just sit around and do nothing."

I try and take a guess at whatever it is she could be feeling so guilty about but nothing comes to mind and I don't push it. Instead I light two cigarettes and hold one out for her to take. She accepts it- places her lips where mine have already been. In a way we are already kissing.

"You do this kind of work before?" she asks, turning on the radio before moving out onto the road.

"Couple of times," I claim, "back in Los Angeles... Usually around Christmas."

She releases an appreciative-sounding whistle. "Los Angeles," she says. "I'd never have guessed that's where you're from."

"It isn't," I tell her, "I just lived there a while."

"So where are you from originally?" she asks.

"Small town out in the middle of nowhere. I left when I was young," I tell her. "I remember it being a lot better than this place but I guess it could be just as shitty now, if not worse."

"You really don't talk like I'd expect you to," she laughs.

"It depends on who's around," I shrug. "I have my *respectful manner* for some people and I'm how I am around other people... People I feel comfortable with."

"I get that," Liz says, "we act how we're expected to act."

"Everyone's a bullshitter," I sigh.

Liz smiles in agreement and takes a pull on her cigarette. Without taking her eyes from the road she briefly points at the radio and says, "You can change the station if you want."

"It's fine the way it is."

"You like Dinosaur Junior?"

"I don't know," I ask, "who are they?"

"They're playing right now!" she laughs.

"Oh," I smirk. "I was never one to really get into music."

"Seriously? Who do you listen to?"

"I don't really listen to anybody," I explain, "only ever what other people have put on around me. With my mom it was The Beatles; a friend of mine liked The Brian Jonestown Massacre, but I couldn't really tell you who was playing if we were in a bar or watching the TV."

"That's just so *alien*," she says. "What about shows? Who was the last person you went to see?"

"I don't know," I shrug. "I've been in places where local bands have played but that's about it."

"Get out of here!"

"What?" I chuckle nervously.

"There isn't one rock band or singer you really wanted to see?"

"No," I say. "Never really liked the idea of going... Getting there early to get near the stage, trying to ignore how desperate you are for a piss, or getting there to be by the bar and toilets but you can't make out the person playing... People desperate to get by? What's the point about that?" I ask her, "Where's the enjoyment?"

"Now you sound a little like a man in your profession should," she jokes, stopping at a red. "Did you know I was in a band? Even played Los Angeles a couple of times."

"I'd have come to watch you," I tell her.

"Thanks," she laughs.

"What were you called?"

"The Upright Cats," she says. "Private joke. But I was on bass and backing vocals."

"You have anything of a following?"

"Sure," she nods as the lights go from red to amber to green. "We had a record deal and everything," she says, putting her foot back down.

"That's pretty impressive."

"I think so, too," she says. "We supported a couple of big bands, played a few festivals while on tour. It was fun for a while."

"What went wrong?"

"A couple of things," she says, "it's why I left."

"What happened to the others?"

"They're still together. The tour I walked out on is still going, I think."

"Wait a minute," I ask, "so this is all recent history for you?"

"Yeah," she nods.

I lean back in my seat and ask, "You miss it?"

"Parts of it," she admits. "And I shouldn't have just bailed on my friends like I did but I was in a bad place."

I decide it best to leave it at that for the moment.

8

Liz drops the speed to a crawl with preparing to stop the van outside a three-storey building with large windows at the front; TRYFORDS CENTER FOR THE DEAF spelled out in reflective letters up high on the wall. There are a couple of vans already parked up front; L. Rinder's Catering written in bold letters along the side and beneath this, in smaller letters, a list of things they cater for. Parties. Private functions. Weddings. Bar Mitzvahs. Graduation ceremonies. Business meetings and more.

Each one of the vans has a young guy leaning against the driver's door, smoking a cigarette. They've parked in such a neat little line and so close together you can see it's easy for them to hold a conversation without having to take a step closer to one another. College boys making a little extra money and hoping on doing little work.

"They working with us?" I ask.

"No," Liz says with a shake of her head. "They'll help us get everything ready and then they won't be around until we want to close up."

She makes her way to the back of the line. The boys offer a polite wave as she passes and it makes me feel a little jealous. Both of them have a good build- it's possible they got into college under a football scholarship- and their features are smooth. Never a bone broken. I wouldn't put it past either one of them to take off their jacket, supposedly because of the heat, and reveal an Upright Cats t-shirt. Because who wouldn't hit on Liz?

"What about the people who'll be coming for something to eat?"

"Give them an hour," she says, "it won't get busy until dark. A lot of them," she explains, "live in town and haven't had a pay rise or even a steady income in a long time. They're struggling but they don't want the neighbours to know they're struggling."

"What about the homeless? You know any of their stories?"

"Banks took possession of their home during the crash," she says, parking the van. "Some will arrive early and then rush over to the building to definitely get a room; others will turn up late and offer to help out, knowing we'll try and squeeze them in even if all rooms have been taken."

"You want a smoke before we go in?" I ask, hoping to keep her to myself for just a few minutes longer.

"Sure," she smiles, "take one of mine this time," she adds, taking a pack of *Something-or-Other* Lites from her pocket. She hands a smoke to me and I thank her, searching for my light while she waits for the van's cigarette lighter to heat up.

"Lights are terrible for your health," I say, lighting up. "You bring the smoke deeper inside your lungs," I reveal, handing my light over. She accepts instead of waiting for the van to give her what she wants.

"Get out of town," she says.

"Honest truth," I go on, "only gets any worse if you smoke menthols."

She nods, blows smoke from her nostrils on handing my Zippo back to me. "My dad used to smoke cigars," she says, "big ones. Used to go through them like they were cigarettes. I tried one when I was ten or eleven and barfed all over the dining room. My brother said my skin was a greenish-blue."

"A brother," I smile, "older or younger?"

"Two minutes older," she says, "twins. We're not identical."

"So you got all the looks?"

"But he got all the brains," she laughs. "He owns a chain of hardware stores. You'd be surprised how much money he makes. People are always wanting to improve home security or put up a shelf."

"Paint a fence..."

"The list is endless," she chuckles. "When we got a record deal," she says, looking down at her feet before raising her head to look out of her side window, "we talked and talked until they give us a lot of money," she smiles, "and we thought we were made for life because of it. Nobody had said you have to pay it back before you get paid again!" she laughs. "You're touring and doing all kinds of promotional work and all the money you're making is to pay back the advance you were given. You ask for a little money to survive the week and the money you owe shoots right back up again. If somebody had explained to me how it worked, I'd have asked for a bare minimum."

One of the college boys appears beside her door before I have the chance to say anything to that. He's smiling, his teeth all straight and brilliantly white and his hair has both volume and control. I bet he'd be exactly what I was looking for if I'd been born a girl.

"Liz," he grins, "why aren't we invited to your party?"

"You couldn't keep up at my pace," she jokes before going into the introductions. "Lee," she says, "this is Terry. Terry, Lee."

"What's up?" he says with a nod. "My boy over there is Peter. He's great," he quips, "so long as you ignore him asking for money."

"Right," Liz laughs, "and what about you?"

"Me? I'm straight up and down," he grins. "So what's the plan for tonight?"

"Well," Liz says, "me and Lee are going to have one more smoke to give you two boys time to get everything ready and then we'll all go inside. As far as plans go," she laughs, "I think it's pretty tight."

Terry grins and says, "Tighter than a nun's snatch," before looking to me and adding, "no offence."

"Don't worry about it," I tell him, wondering whether he's simply trying to see how far he can shove me or out to impress Liz at my expense.

"Get outta here," Liz tells him with a smirk, "get everything ready for tonight's show."

"On my way," he says, performing a mock-salute before turning to head back to his van and his friend.

"I'm sorry about him," Liz says, handing me a cigarette, "he thinks he's a lot funnier than he is."

"Nothing to worry about," I tell her. "You know him well?"

"I only met him through doing this," she says. "I usually have a couple of drinks with them when we've finished here."

I ask her, "You drinking with them tonight?"

"Probably," she says. "You coming along?"

"I can't," I sigh. "Money's a problem for the foreseeable future."

"Don't worry about it," she grins, "I'll shout you some. Well," she adds, "my older brother with his regular deposits into my bank account will, but you get what I mean."

"You blow all your song royalties?"

"Please," she smiles, "it'll be years before the record company is willing to pay me any of those."

9

WE SIT MAKING small talk but it's hard to stay focused because of Peter and Terry. They act like kids as they're unloading the vans, shoving one another and laughing as they roll shining chests of stainless steel on wheels towards the deaf place. It's like watching them bring out a complete portable kitchen. I hadn't been expecting so much stuff. The sight of it has me regretting the fact I came along because it looks like there could be a whole lot of work to get done.

"That's a lot of stuff," I sigh.

"It looks worse than it is," Liz says, "you've got your soups and your warm bread rolls and your plates and spoons but that's about it. They just want the serving counter to be a lot bigger than necessary. It's to stop people knocking into each other while they're waiting."

I ask, "And does it work?"

"Most of the time," she smiles. "As long as no one turns up too drunk."

"I thought the Missionaries turned back drunks?"

"They won't give them a place to stay but they're welcome to come and get a bite to eat."

"Any of the men ever hit on you?" I ask with a grin.

"Sometimes," she says, "but the ones who know Abigail are too scared."

A new song starts on the radio and Liz excitedly turns up the volume. I hadn't been paying attention to the radio- had clearly forgot it was on- but she hadn't. Do I really not interest her at all?

"I love this song," she says.

"Who is it?"

Show a woman you're willing to learn from them, to be moulded by them, and you might just become more interesting to them.

"Ladyhawke," she says.

"Like the film?" I ask her just to show I do know *some* things.

"Yeah," Liz says, "it's where she got the name from," and just like that I now know Ladyhawke isn't a band but a woman. I think.

"You ever play with her?"

Liz shakes her head. "No," she says, "saw her play once but I can't really remember it. I was drunk and I used to dabble in things that aren't too good for you."

I want to snatch the collar from my throat and tell her everything... Tell her how fucked me and Doyle used to get on prescription pills we'd lifted or bartered for... Tell her of the times me and Cole were up way after the early hours with a mountain of coke in front of us... But I don't. I just gently pat her leg and say, "Just remember you can be whatever you want to be. A girl like you could achieve whatever she wanted and have any man lucky enough to catch her eye."

"That's everything in place," she says like she didn't hear me, eyes on Peter and Terry as they turn around to face us from the front of the building with the contents of their vans ready and waiting. "I can't promise you'll enjoy the next couple of hours but I'll definitely buy you a drink or two for coming along."

I follow her like a loyal puppy, trying to work out whether she's giving me mixed signals- whether she's sending me any signals at all or if it's just in my bruised skull- and stop at the building alongside her. Terry and Peter step aside with a smile to let her near the intercom on the wall beside the door. The sight of it alone is enough to make me chuckle a little louder than I'd intended. Liz turns back to me with a smile and an arched eyebrow. "What's so funny?" she asks.

"It's a deaf-house," I explain, "and they want you to ring the bell."

Liz smiles, shakes her head a little, turning back and holds her finger down on the button a little while. A static response comes before a disembodied man's voice. "Yes?"

"It's Liz and the gang."

"Just a minute- I'll come let you in."

"It's the door," Liz explains, "it has to be opened manually because of a fault."

"Right," I nod. "Who is it coming to let us in?"

"Bobby," she says. "He's something of the security guard around this place."

"Right," Peter smirks, "it's just he has a habit of disappearing if an argument ever starts up. I'd feel better with Martin around. He's pretty-much the janitor," he adds for my benefit, "or the nearest thing a forgotten building like this shithole has to one."

Bobby opens the door for us. He's tall and as thin as a rake. If there's a rule in place about not smoking on the job he isn't paying it any attention because a cigar that's only a little thicker than a cigarette is in his hand. It's thin but the smell of it is impossible to ignore. "Liz," he says with a smile wide enough to show the gold tooth he has near the back of his mouth, "is it *that* time of the week again already?"

"Sure is," she says before giving him a quick hug. "This is Lee," she says, pointing back to me, "and you know the two stooges already."

"Lee," he says, stepping out to shake me by the hand, "you from the Missionaries?"

"That's exactly where I'm from," I smile.

"But you're new in town, right?"

Peter says, "He's the one my uncle found out on the road."

I look back at him, then to Terry and eventually Liz. "You never told me that," is all I can think of saying right now.

"Damn," Bobby says to win back my attention, "I never even thought! I mean," he continues, "I can see the bruising but I knew a priest and he used to get into the ring in his free time- do a little sparring. I thought it might have been something you did."

"Only from time to time," I grin, making out I'm comfortable here and we're all good friends. The truth of the matter is I'm curious to why Liz didn't tell me about how I'm connected to the catering boys already.

"Only from time to time," Bobby chuckles back. "Anyway," he says, "I'm keeping you out there like you have the plague or something. Come on in, come on in."

Liz is the first to enter with Terry and Peter stepping aside to make sure I go in after her so they can trail in from behind with the first of the catering equipment. And it's funny, because the corridor I step into just has me feeling like I'm back in Saint Claire's even though it doesn't resemble the place in the slightest but it weirds me out. The walls and ceiling feel to be moving in a couple of inches and I find myself pulling at the collar around my throat to try and make it easier for me to breathe, my heart beating like the wings of a hummingbird.

"Is there a bathroom I can use?" I ask, hoping I don't sound as nervous to the others as I do myself. Liz stops and turns back to look at me without an ounce of concern on her face but Bobby goes on walking ahead in a slow, easy pace. "Sure," he says back to me, "just through that door there."

I move forward as quickly as I can without sprinting, moving past Liz to reach the door that the always reliable Bobby had pointed at without turning to look first. She asks, "You feeling okay?"

"Sure," I tell her, "just a bit of a dizzy spell."

I push the door inwards and stumble into the restroom with my eyes locking onto the unlocked door of the nearest stall like they had known it was there long before I did and I'm rushing on ahead, arm stretched out for that second door when I spot Doyle coming in alongside me. I gasp in amazement, because I must have taken his pulse wrong or something and left him to be found and taken to a nearby hospital where he remained until he woke up again but when I turn to face him he isn't there. And I stand there, my heart still beating like crazy, just staring at my reflection in the mirror on the wall. Even when I'm looking right at my own image, it's difficult for me to know who I'm looking at, who's looking back at me, and it isn't just the bruising or the nose, it's more than that. I can't tell whether it's Lee I'm looking to or Doyle.

I hear wheels rattle along the corridor outside as Peter and Terry take their shit to, well, wherever.

"Don't get all deep on me," I mutter, moving towards the

sink with ideas of splashing cold water over my face, "you're nowhere near smart enough to understand."

The water trickles out, discoloured and lukewarm. Standing this close to the mirror, you can't ignore the handprints. Open hands; marks to show where reflections have tried pushing their way onto the other side of the glass.

10

WE SET UP camp in the largest room on the first floor. There are already plenty of tables and chairs set up; the whole layout reminding me of my time in prison. Terry and Peter start putting all of the equipment they're in charge of into an L shape. Bobby talks to Liz about the little things; how many people is she expecting to turn up? Does she think some won't come because it's cold?

He even asks if she's working it alone tonight even though I'm here, keeping an eye over everybody and trying not to let on how uncomfortable I've been feeling because Doyle's on my mind. I can't help but picture him, left to rot on that park bench... Maybe even cremated, his ashes in a misplaced urn now because nobody knew anything about the guy. Nobody but me, anyway.

I hear Liz tell him there's been a slight change of schedule and Barbara will be turning up to lend a hand. I try to put a face to the name but come up blank.

"So how're you feeling?" Peter asks me.

"Oh," I say, "a lot better, thanks. So it was your uncle that found me?"

"Yeah," he nods, "said you'd been hit by a car. You get a look at the make?"

"No," I tell him, "it's all a bit of a blur."

"It would be," he says in understanding. "He'll be glad to know you're doing well."

"Could you thank him for me?"

"Sure," he says, "no problem."

"He thinks he's entitled to three wishes," Terry calls out to me with a dumb smirk on his face, "tell them they're for his uncle!"

"So what's your uncle's name?" I ask like I didn't hear Terry's latest attempt at humour.

"Alec."

"Alec?" I grin and ask, "He isn't a writer, is he?"

"What?" Peter smiles back at me, obviously puzzled by the question, and says, "He's a courier; he delivers letters for a lawyer. Did somebody tell you he was a writer?"

"No," I explain, "just thinking of somebody I met a while back. I wouldn't have thought Alec was a common name."

"I don't think it is," he says, "I've never met a second one."

"Well," I smile, "they're out there. But what's the plan," I ask, "we all going out once we're done here?"

"Sure," he nods. "We usually take everything back to the shop and Liz takes the van back to the Missionaries and we meet over at one of the bars. They're not great," he says, "Tryfords doesn't have much to offer but they're pretty cheap and they'll get you drunk."

"Sometimes that's all you really need in life," I tell him.

"You know it," he smirks. "But how're you finding the place, anyway?"

"Tryfords? It seems nice," I reply with a casual shrug, "but there's something I've got to ask you about the Missionaries."

He gives me a quizzical look and says, "Go on..."

"Well," I smirk, "are they part of a church or is it just a business?"

"I don't get you," he says.

It's my time to smirk now. "Are they basically charity workers in Halloween getups?"

Peter laughs at that and Terry, busy locking the wheels of one of his containers into place, looks over at us. Only briefly but it's enough for me to know he's a little worried about how he might be missing out on something interesting.

"I can't help you out on that one," Peter says, "I just cart shit over here for them. You could maybe ask Liz? She's been with them a while now."

"Yeah," I tell him, "I suppose you're right."

"But what about you," he asks, "you don't think they're legit or something?"

"Forget I mentioned it."

Peter nods and looks to his watch. "You're the boss," he says.

"I don't know if I should head outside for a smoke or just light up in here... It could be my last chance of getting some fresh air for a few hours."

"Outside," I tell him, "I'll join you and you can give me a little more information on the place."

"It'll cost you. Nah," he grins, "I'm just yanking you. Let's go."

11

Barbara - a woman aged someplace between thirty and fifty turns up in her penguin outfit and offers a thin smile to us all, saying how good it is for her to see so many people willing to help those in need. She smiles at me and her eyes narrow a little. Right away I figure Abigail has sent her here to keep an eye on me. It's strange because I can't remember seeing her during my time there, not even once, and I wonder if Abigail put a call in to Tony and Tony sent somebody down from head office to put the feelers out on me.

"It's a pleasure to meet you," I say, stepping forward and offering her my hand, "I really appreciate what the Missionaries are doing in towns like this one."

"It's nothing," she grins, "we do what we were sent here for. Elizabeth," she says, turning away from me, "you've come along so far. Just look at you," she gushes, "rosy cheeks and a sparkle in your eyes. Or is it something in the water?" she quips, turning her attention to the three local men.

Terry smirks, mumbles something into Peter's ear and looks to the latest arrival. "I heard the building you're in used to be a gentleman's club," he says with a straight face, "and a stripper OD'd there. Down in the basement," he says, "and they only ever found her because of the smell."

12

MEN LOOKING FOR a free meal start filling the place really fast. There doesn't look to be a single woman among them; just broken and dirty-looking guys without an ounce of hope left in them. They're quiet and they look nervous, falling into the orderly line and waiting to be served before finding a chair to sit in. Barbara, proud of her fake nails ending in a blunt, square cut is all smiles handing over the bread rolls but I keep spotting her true self every time she glances over at me, which is a lot. She's not offended at how I've put myself on the far side of the room, leaning against a wall with my arms folded over my chest, but something else. Maybe a fraud recognises a fraud, maybe she has doubts to my having no money.

Terry and Peter are sitting at a table they have claimed for themselves, the two playing cards and talking with broad smiles but it's impossible for me to make out what they're saying. It doesn't bother me anyway. I'm feeling bored more than anything else. Wondering just when I should head out for a smoke, I spot him getting up from his chair and making his way to the door he came in through. Just seeing him is enough to stop my breathing for a moment.

Owen.

The man responsible for my leaving Doyle first time around. The man Doyle told me had died once Aids was too much for him to take.

Owen heading for the exit without a care in the world, wiping his mouth on the back of his hand. He's even ditched the shoes he'd kept together with sticky-tape all those years back.

"Owen," I mutter to myself and then he's out on the corridor and out of sight.

I rush out after him, ignoring Barbara as she watches me with interest. Liz, being Liz, is too preoccupied in helping the needy to notice me.

He heads down the stairs and drops out of sight for a second time. I reach the top of the stairs just in time to lose him behind a wall.

"Fuck," I hiss. I go on chasing, jumping down two, three stairs at a time.

When I'm down on the corridor, he's nowhere to be seen. There isn't a fucking trace of him and there's no way he would have gotten out the door without my hearing him. The only place he could be would be

"The bathroom..."

13

He's standing with his back to me, pissing in the urinal with his free hand pressed against the wall. I let the door silently close behind me and just stand there, waiting. He finishes, shakes himself off and turns to head for the sink. He jumps a little, realizing how he isn't alone but shakes it off soon enough. He doesn't particularly break his stride. It's the collar around my neck. It has that effect on people.

"Good evening," he says, "Father...?"

He sounds happy for a man a decade or so dead.

"Reverend," I correct him. My voice is a lot quieter than I'd been prepared for... Weaker, even. "Reverend Doyle," I say a lot louder to make up for it.

"Sure was a good turnout you had tonight," he says, watching the dirty water as it trickles from the tap and runs down the drain. For a moment he just goes on watching, trying to decide whether he should rinse his hands off or not. In the ends he decides to. The man doesn't even think it important to say how he knew someone by my name a long time ago.

"You come here often?"

"When I can," he says.

"You live in town?"

"Naw," he says with a shake of his head, "just out of it. Few of us here tonight live on the field just off A71. You seen it?"

"No," I tell him.

"It's a nice place," he says, shaking his hands as he sidesteps to the container where the paper towels are kept. Or *were* kept. "Built our own shelters," he goes on, first realizing his fingers can't feel any towels and then tipping his head to one side so he can look inside the container just to be sure. "You're welcome to drop by any time you like," he says, turning to face me with a grin as he wipes his hands dry against oily jeans.

There doesn't look to be a single tooth left along the bottom of

42

his mouth and the top isn't much better. Four or so on top, one next to the other, all orange and fragile-looking.

"How long have you been there?"

"Years," he says like he's real proud of it. "Cops used to come and knock down our places but they gave up once they had to admit we only rebuilt them!"

I ask him, "How's it compare to Los Angeles?"

"How do you mean?"

"Where you're staying," I say, "how does it compare to Los Angeles?"

"I don't know," he shrugs, managing to pull off a look of mild confusion. "What makes you ask that?"

He tries to back away as I move towards him but once his back is pressed against the tiled wall he has no choice but to admit he's got no place to run. He holds his hands up in surrender and gasps as I take a tight hold of his jacket and pull him just a matter of inches from my face.

"What happened?" I want to know, "Did he kick you out or did you take everything he had to give and bail?"

"Take it easy, buddy," he says on dropping his hands onto my wrists. He doesn't try to pull free; he just keeps his hands where they are to stop me from throwing a punch without first giving him a little warning. "I don't know what you think you heard but-"

I take a step back and bring him with me, just so I can force him back against the wall.

Doyle told me Owen was dead and here he is, right in front of me.

He isn't Owen. If he was, one of the few teeth he had left in his mouth would have had an all too recognisable hole right at the front. And then there's the eyes... I can't put my finger on it but they're a little different. I'm fucking sure of it.

"Brother," he pleads, "I don't know what all this is about but you can sort this whole mess out by talking with Terry! Talk to him already," he begs, "it's got to be a misunderstanding we have here!"

The man is Owen. The man isn't Owen.

"Terry?"

"Sure," he says, "Terry'll vouch for me," he says like that would mean a thing to me.

The man is Owen.

The man isn't Owen.

"Get out of here," I sigh, letting my hands fall free.

He doesn't need to be told twice. He rushes out of the bathroom. I hear him grunt to someone on his way out but don't turn back to see *who*. I just lean against the sink a while, head bowed and eyes watching the slow trickle of brown water. More than anything right now, I need a smoke. Interrogating Terry can wait. I run a little water over my fingers before running them through my hair; gather my composure and make my way back out onto the corridor.

Barbara.

She's right outside the door with a look of satisfaction on her face. It makes her look cruel.

"Mr Doyle," she says, "is anything the matter?"

"Not really," I tell her, "I'm just about to head out for a cigarette."

"Yes," she says, falling in alongside me as I head for the exit whilst easing the cigarettes from my pocket, "you've worked well, it's understandable you'd want a quick break."

We head outside and see the black guy I'd had pressed against the wall rushing away from the place. I act like he's no interest to me, open the pack of cigarettes in my hand and see how few I have to my name.

"What do you make of what we're doing here?" Barbara asks, taking a pack of her own from a hidden pocket somewhere on her getup. She takes one for herself before giving me the chance to take one of my own. They're menthol and they're *lites*. They would be, wouldn't they?

I take one anyway, just to help my own last a little longer.

"You do your best," I answer, lighting up returning the Zippo to my side pocket without offering her a go at the flame. "We all need to help people to help themselves."

"Quite," she says, never once taking her eyes from the back of the retreating black guy. She lights her cigarette with a match, dropping it to the gutter once it has served its purpose. "It pains me to say it but others would take advantage of such a place."

"They sure would."

"Our poor friend you met in the bathroom could be helped if it wasn't for other influences. *Internal* influences," she says.

"What're you trying to say?"

"I only heard a snippet of your discussion but I heard Terry's name being mentioned."

I relax hearing that and shrug my shoulders. "Just a man throwing a name around," I tell her.

"Or a man in need being taken advantage of by someone there to help."

"I don't think I follow."

Barbara looks right at me as she takes the longest drag on her cigarette you could imagine, it's like she's going for the world record or something. She just goes on looking right at me, never blinking, just sucking and sucking on that damn thing until she finally pulls it free from her withered lips. "You know how places like our own run," she says, clearly mistaking me for somebody else, "and you know budget restraints prevent us from looking into our volunteers as much as we would like to and men like Terry will take advantage of that."

"Right," I answer with a knowing smile and a nod, "I get you. It took me all of five minutes to see through him but I couldn't get the guy who just left to tell me anything."

"Well, I don't expect you to perform miracles," she laughs, "but keep an open eye on him, would you? That little son of a bitch is up to no good but no one else seems able to see it."

I want to ask her how many *Hail Marys* she'll be doing to make up for the colourful language but keep myself from doing so. Making light will only see me losing a little of the shine she now seems so happy to put all over me.

"There's a cop I know out in LA," I claim, "and he could spot a guilty man with his eyes closed but you know how people lie, right? Every once in I while," I tell her, "he'd call me and ask me to get over to the station. I'd walk into the interview room and the man on the other side of the desk would take one look at me and confess *everything*. The ones that didn't," I finish, "I still knew from taking one quick look at them whether they were guilty or godless."

Barbara nods, drops her cigarette to the floor and presses her foot down on it like she's pretending it's Terry's pecker beneath her weight.

"I've enjoyed getting to know you," she says. "I'm going to tell Abigail it might be an idea to have you around for a while."

14

I KEEP MY eyes on Terry and Peter as they go about loading the vans up. Liz takes her cigarettes out, picks two from the pack and hands one to me. She told me we didn't have to do any of the brushing up because Martin would be arriving soon enough to clear up the little mess left over, so I've no idea why we're waiting on Terry and Peter instead of just arranging to meet them somewhere. No idea why we're waiting on them but I'm sort of glad we are because I want to see Terry in the act of doing *something*.

"Thanks," I tell her, flicking my Zippo open. I light my own before holding the flame close enough for her to use. She thanks me and blows a little smoke from her lips and out of the window beside her.

"What did you think?"

"You run a smooth ship," I say to answer her question. "Everybody there clearly thinks you're approachable. That's always a good thing."

"Did Barbara ask for your life story?"

"No," I tell her, "and it's probably for the best because she'd only have doubted every word I said. She just wanted to know if I had any juicy gossip from Los Angeles. She left pretty disappointed. Is she here often?" I ask.

"Not really. If a tile on the roof needs replacing or if the store down the street charges a penny extra for a carton of milk then she's straight down to investigate but that's about it. I'm guessing she's only here now to make sure everybody's still working without Antony being around."

"Yeah," I nod, "probably. Are you sure you don't mind shouting me a few beers tonight?"

"Not at all," she grins. "If I can't rely on a preacher to keep me out of trouble, who will?"

"That's the answer to find. But Terry and Peter are coming

with us, right?"

Liz nods and blows a faint trail of smoke from her mouth. "Feed the five hundred and then get yourself at least one strong drink," she says, "it's something of a tradition."

"There are worse ones to have. You know what either one of them do when they're not working here?"

"I don't know," she shrugs, "I guess they're just catering other parts of town."

"Men of mystery," I chuckle. "You know anything about them?"

"Like what?" she laughs.

"I don't know," I say like I'm trying to think of something, "how about their names?"

"Terry Docherty," she answers proudly. "I know that because he showed me his payslip one time because he thought he'd been underpaid."

"What about Peter?" I ask to keep her from growing suspicious.

"Peter," she says, "Peter... I don't know, I'm pretty sure he's never told me."

"Maybe he has but you find him too boring to listen to," I joke.

The two finish what they had to do and walk over to the van together. Liz winds her window down a little more. "You done?" she asks even though it's clear to see they are.

"Just have to take the stuff back," Peter answers. "Where're we meeting?"

"I don't know," she says, "how about Thingwall's?"

"Thingwall's it is," Peter says with an easy nod, "see you there."

"See you," she says, starting the engine and we begin the journey back to the Missionaries before either one of them are back in their van. Why we insisted on waiting for them only becomes a bigger mystery to me because of it.

"One of the girls will drive the van back for me tomorrow," Liz says to me, "so we're pretty much getting back there and shooting right back out again."

"We don't have to be back for curfew, do we?" I smile.

"Don't worry," she grins, "I haven't found a lock I couldn't pick."

It's a joke, it must have been a joke, but it still helps her come over as all dangerous and sexy.

15

"Pretty unusual name, isn't it?" I ask, holding the door open for Liz to walk in ahead of me. I need her to lead the way seeing how she's paying for the drinks.

"A little," she smiles, "but the prices are good."

Thingwall's is a small bar in the basement of a large building. If that has you picturing the bar from *Cheers* then you're picturing it all wrong. There's a drugstore just beyond the ceiling, a much larger drugstore than Walt's, and it looks like sedated zombies came down here the second they had collected their prescriptions. Pale-skinned men with thinning hair and worn clothes sitting at the bar in silence. A pool table in the farthest corner, cues on the table, and a solitary old geezer with a chair placed beside it with hopes of talking whoever comes over to enjoy a game to take him on first. It takes me a while to notice the boys manning the bar because of all these things. They're all tattoos and Elvis Presley haircuts; fading black t-shirts with *Thingwall's* stencilled across the chest in solid white. They somehow give the impression that this place used to be *the* place.

"What's your poison?" Liz asks, taking a purse from her brown leather over-the-shoulder bag. It's not a handbag but it isn't a satchel.

"I'll have what you're having," I reply because a barman is already in front of us and I'm forced to admit I spent too long trying to settle on a name for her bag than looking at the available drinks on display.

"Two house rums and coke," she says, holding two fingers up for the barman to avoid any confusion, "two bottles of Bud."

"Ice?"

"No thanks," she says with a shake of her head before turning to ask if I would like a little ice in my drink after all.

"It'd only get in the way," I say back at her with a smile. She turns to tell the barman my preference but he's already fixing the drinks, scooping ice cubes from a plastic drawer behind the bar and dropping them into one of the two glasses. I ask Liz, "Are you allowed to smoke in here?"

"Of course," she says, "but they expect you to stand across the street if you go outside for a smoke and you can't take one into the restrooms. Don't ask me why."

"I won't," I grin.

The barman slides two bottles of Bud and two large glasses of house rum and coke (one *with* ice) in front of her. She hands over a note, tells him to keep the change and he thanks her for it before turning away, money into the cash register and then he's straight onto the next customer.

"Come on," Liz says, "we'll go get some songs on the jukebox."

I hadn't even noticed it on first entering, now I wonder how I missed it. The look of it has me thinking of a baby's coffin mixed with pieces of an old computer lifted from a junkyard. Just approaching it is enough to increase my heart rate. There's no real noise down here so it's more than likely that our choices will start playing as soon as we take to selecting them and if I pick something bad then I'll have to make out it was a joke before it's too late to sound believable.

Liz begins dropping coins into a slot. I watch digital numbers move up in sets of two until she's happy to stop at eight.

"Four each," she says and then she's pressing a button with an arrow pointing to the left on it and what looks like a book made of plastic kept safely behind glass turns a page every time she does, "I'll go first."

"How old are the songs on this?" I ask her.

"It depends," she says as she continues to turn the pages, "all the records are compilations; *Best of the 60s, Best of the 70s, Best rock, Best Rolling Stones...*"

It's the Stones she begins with. I watch her key in the number for Paint It Black and the track begins less than five seconds later, while she's still taking a step to the side to give me a little space, "Your turn."

I swallow and step a little closer, bring a shaking finger to the arrow keys and start turning the pages for myself, terrified her song of choice will finish before I've selected my own. And she had been speaking the truth; I see that with every turn of the page.

Best alt-folk-rock of the 00s.

Best Movie Songs.

I give a sigh of relief on finding The Beatles because you're always safe with The Beatles and I go for Let It Be simply because it's the first song title I see. Liz asks, "You heard the Paul McCartney version of this?" reclaiming her place.

"I thought this *was* Paul McCartney?" I say, already doubting something I've taken as gospel for my entire life.

"There's another version of the entire album," she explains, "McCartney removed all of Phil Spector's input a couple of years back."

"I never heard it. Is it any good?"

She shrugs and says, "I prefer Spector's take," she keys in a song with a title I don't see in record time, stepping back so the ball is in my court all over again.

"Thanks for the drinks," I say, figuring it'll look better for me if she guesses it's taking me a while to select a song because we're in conversation, "I'll be sure to get you some if my wallet ever turns up."

"You had no joy looking for that?"

"No."

"Have you called your bank?"

"Sure have," I lie, "but they won't send a replacement card here because they don't have the Missionaries' address on file. So even if I find my wallet," I sigh, "the card has probably been cancelled already."

I find Sam Cooke and key in the code for Cupid, hoping his serenading will only act to make her melt around me. Stepping to the side I ask her, "Have you ever looked for any of your songs on this?"

"We won't be on it," she laughs. "Some bars have jukeboxes linked to the internet now," she says as if to blow my mind, "and they'll find any song you type into it *and* play the video with it."

"The future is here," I say as if I'm joking.

"Next step is cloning all the dead musicians," she laughs, "and taking the billboards back!"

I laugh but stop making a sound on noticing a black guy in a wheelchair making his way to the bar. He's wearing a purple velvet suit but it's his legs that really capture my attention. They're swollen stumps that are too short to even hang over the seat, ending in feet like boulders. White socks on show are being stretched to the max they're that big and the black sneakers he's sporting must have been made especially for him. Liz spots him and giggles. "Damn," she says, "only just seen he's here- I would have gone for Purple Rain if I'd known earlier; you should see him play air guitar to that!"

"Who is he?" I ask.

"His name's Leroy," she says, "I think. We have no idea how he gets in and out of here, no idea if he even knows anybody or just tries to join up with different people during the night. We were drinking tequila one night," she goes on, "and Pete starting writing on the table with salt and Leroy told the barmen we were vandalising the place! Can you believe that?"

"No," I say, watching him order a cocktail pitcher and one tall glass, "that does sound pretty bizarre."

"*Bizarre*," she laughs, "good word to pick right as I'm keying in The Doors! Jim Morrison said he felt *bizarre* the night he died."

16

PETER AND TERRY arrive right as we're settling down in a free booth having selected all of our songs. Terry is laughing and looking to the untrained eye like a man who has drank enough to be feeling a pretty decent buzz. To eyes like my own it's easy to know it's not drink at all but something else. A little granulated happiness being the most likely explanation.

"Beat us here," he says to Liz as Peter waits to be served at the bar. "What is that?" he asks lifting my rum to take a sniff at it while dropping in beside us. "Is that rum? I thought people in your profession kept to wine," he jokes, placing my drink back down.

"Only on the holidays."

"Only on the holidays," he laughs. "So Barbara is in town again?" he says to Liz with a grin. "I thought my balls felt like somebody was squeezing them a little too hard."

"She not fond of you?" I ask before Liz has a chance to change the topic of conversation.

"Has a beef with me," Terry says, lighting a cigarette and rolling his eyes. "I was born and raised in *this* town," he adds pressing his hand down against the table top, "she's from wherever and I can count the number of times she has been here on *one* hand and she has a problem with me. You know something else? I was volunteering for the Missionaries a good period before she even turned up to look around for the first time but she decided she had a problem with me there and then. Never admitted it but she doesn't have to, it's obvious. It's all jealousy," he claims, "she's jealous of how I interact with the others and the people who turn up for something to eat."

"What's your take on the Missionaries?"

He lifts his chin for a second to blow smoke up toward the ceiling. "What do you mean?" he asks.

"I'm just asking you the same question I asked your boy Peter over there; you think they act nice but pocket a lot of money from the government instead of putting it all back to the people they're supposed to be helping?"

Terry looks to Liz and makes an exaggerated smile as he opens his eyes real wide. "Liz," he laughs, "is this an undercover reporter we have here? You're the man of God," he says to me, "you should know frauds from the real thing... What's your impression?"

"Still trying to figure it out," I shrug, lighting a cigarette. "Abigail wanted me gone but Barbara is going to suggest I stay a little longer to keep an eye on you."

Liz turns to me in surprise and says, "You're kidding?"

"I told you!" Terry laughs, "I told you! So what're you going to do?" He asks me, "You going to pretend to be my friend so you can get the intel on me? You going to be all Donnie Darko?"

"Donnie *Brasco*," Peter says with a sigh. He places a drink down on the table for Terry but keeps hold of his own on sitting down.

"Whatever," Terry smirks. "You thinking of infiltrating my organisation and uncovering all the secret plans for world domination? Try it," he laughs, "I Déjà Dairé you."

"Pornstar," Peter explains for my benefit. I notice Liz looks a little disappointed, like she doesn't want to know the people she's hoping to find redemption through could be nothing more than phonies, but I ignore it for the moment. I don't have it in me to tell her you can only find true redemption via God and if He is real, it's more than likely he has no idea she even exists.

"Only thing I want to find is a good time," I shrug, offering a sigh to go with it so Terry will know I'm tired of him already. "Missionaries have me doing unpaid work to keep a roof over my head and Abigail is in such a hurry to get rid of me that she has me using a woman's deodorant and shaving with a pink razor, so it's not like I owe them anything."

"Get this," Liz says to change the subject once and for all, "Lee has no real interest in music."

"You must like *something*," Peter says with a disbelieving grin.

"Doesn't go to live shows or buy records," Liz adds to prove her point.

Peter asks me, "Is that true?"

"Pretty much," I tell him.

"Man," he says, "that's pretty out there. The music you listen to is the soundtrack to your life, you know?"

"Fucking stoner!" Terry laughs, throwing an arm around Peter's shoulders and drawing him in close. "Listen to the stoner talk! Peter here once took acid and was convinced they were going to use two buildings in town to plug us directly into the moon once we'd used all of our natural resources!"

"Shut up," Peter laughs, pushing Terry off of him. "He's just yanking your chain," he tells me, "he thinks shit like that is funny. Sorry for the language," he adds before drinking a little beer from the bottle.

A good mood takes hold of the entire table. I wait for Liz to be heading the bathroom and Terry to be waiting at the bar before turning to Peter and saying, "Fun night." It's small talk I don't really have the time for but if it has to, it can hopefully be counted for the next time it comes down to just the two of us.

"Yeah," Peter nods in agreement, "I wouldn't mind staying here but Terry and Liz will want to be heading somewhere else soon."

"Alone?" I ask him, "Are they together?"

"No," he smirks, "I just meant they'll want to go someplace a little cooler."

I nod in pretend understanding. "I ask you something?" I say, keeping my eyes on Terry.

"Sure," he replies easily. "Go for it."

"What's with Terry?"

"What do you mean?"

"I'm getting the impression he's on more than beer tonight. Toilet breaks of his are more than a little regular."

"Put it down to a hyperactive bladder," Peter shrugs.

"Come on," I say, "man, we're all here for a good time, am I right? If it's because I can't afford to pay then I'm cool with that but if it's not, you can trust me. I'm a man of God," I joke, "remember?"

He looks at me for a second, looks away to stare at a random spot on the wall as he brings an almost empty bottle of beer to his lips. "You're barking up the wrong tree," he says.

"So it's Terry I should be talking to right now? I would," I tell him, "but I don't think he trusts me."

"I have no idea what you're talking about," he smirks, shaking his head so I decide it's time to throw my cards down on the table in a desperate bid for his trust.

"Your uncle found me on a quiet stretch of road where a bunch of good old boys ditched me after handing me my ass on a plate," I sigh. "He thought it had been a hit and run and I went along with that because it beat explaining the kicking I had got. Over a college girl," I claim with a smile, "never could resist them."

He slowly brings the bottle back to his mouth and gives me a look that could be read as meaning *Why are you telling me this?* but I'm more than confident that it's his way of silently asking me to spill a little more.

"Think about it," I tell him, "I'd have got a little money to my name by now if I had a name with any fucking meaning. My wallet and all my bank cards and all my ID isn't left out on a lonely stretch of road because I don't have anything like that. Between the two of us," I smile, leaning in closer, "I'm not long out of prison for a number of home burglaries and one case of assault. Made an exit without a word. The collar on my neck means nothing to me, it's just a stage prop a friend inspired me to use and that's why I haven't even taken the time to let anybody at all know whether it's *reverend* or *father* with me. Why else would I be so suspicious of the Missionaries?" I ask. "A fraud spots a fraud."

Peter downs the final drops of his beer. "This all from the screenplay you're working on?" he smiles.

"Nah," I joke, "my book. You know Walt? Old guy in town, runs his own drugstore?"

Peter laughs. "Let me guess," he says, "head of an organised crime syndicate?"

"I went by his store for the very first time today and you

know what I found out? Zero-three-zero-one," I tell him. "Combination code to get the door open. You'd best believe I want to go back there after hours to figure out a way inside without getting any unwanted attention. Valium can always give me a good feeling. I had a friend who swore by Diazepam but that shit always made me itchy... Gave me cold sweats."

"Holy shit," he chuckles, "what have we here? You're serious, aren't you?"

"I'm just a man looking for an easy life and a free ride."

Liz falls into sight, returning from the bathroom. She drops into the booth and asks, picking up her beer, "What're you two bonding over?"

"Cars," Peter says immediately and like it's no big deal, "Lee has an interest in them. Come on out with me," he says getting to his feet, "you have to look at my baby."

"Whatever you do," Liz says to me from behind an angelic laugh, "do *not* lean on it if you're not fresh out of the bath and wearing clean clothes!"

"I'll keep that in mind," I say, following Peter away from the table, patting Liz's shoulders in parting just so I have an excuse to touch her. Terry spots the two of us heading for the door and shoots Peter a look of interest. Peter puts his hands out in front of him and moves them like they're on the wheel of his car. Terry nods in understanding, turns to the barman who is now ready to take his order.

<h1 style="text-align: center;">17</h1>

I FOLLOW PETER out into the cold night. It's raining. It isn't heavy, more of a drizzle, but there's so much of it falling that everything you see looks like it would on an old TV you couldn't quite tune right.

"There's my girl," Peter says, crossing the road and heading towards a car that would have blended right into man's imagining of the future a long time ago. "1970 Dodge Daytona," he proudly adds, "like Vin Diesel's in the Fast movies."

The car looks midnight black until you get closer to it and realise it's the same kind of dark green as numerous beer bottles.

"How'd you manage to afford this?" I ask.

"My grandpa gave it me," he answers, taking the keys from his back pocket. "He thought it would be good for me to have something to fix-up but when I didn't, he paid for it to be fixed-up for me," he grins, unlocking his door. "Doesn't have all the turbo options like Vin Diesel's but it has a CD player. Get in," he says.

I walk around to the other side of the car and climb in the passenger side, easing the door shut behind me. Peter starts the engine but we don't go anywhere. He starts the engine just so he can use the CD player. Music approaches me from all directions.

"Slade," he says, "one of the best- if not *the* best – rock'n'roll bands to come from England and I'm not just saying that, I fucking mean it."

He reaches under his seat and pulls out a clear plastic bag which is bulging with grass. I'm serious, he's looking at real time if he's ever pulled over with even half of that.

"You deal?"

"No," he says, "I got this off a friend for next to nothing."

"That's a real fucking friend you have there."

"Tell me about it," he laughs, tearing apart a Marlboro so he can get to work rolling a joint. "You smoke grass often?"

"Not as much as I used to," I tell him. "I puked my guts up last time."

"That's a sign you were smoking some nasty shit," he says. "This'll just get you nice and chilled. You'll have a few drinks, have a few laughs and then have the best night's sleep you've had in a long time. I'd rather have this over what Terry's doing tonight," he smirks. "He's taking a mix of tranquilisers for farmyard animals. His bladder's going to shrink down to the size of an apple if he isn't careful."

He licks the gum of his rolling paper, gently moves it between both thumbs and index fingers. The joint is one of the longest I've seen in a long, long time and most definitely the fattest. He lights up and leans back in his seat to get comfortable. Any doubts I had about the quality of his stuff disappears in no time at all because I'm sitting just inches from him but I'm not picking up that pungent stench I usually associate with pot. I find myself feeling more than a little nervous instead. I mean, the last thing I need is for a beat cop to see us and drag us back to the station.

"So what you said back there," he asks, "that the truth?"

"Yeah," I say, grinning because of a nervous fear and not an unshakable confidence in my bullshit and keeping away from the law.

"And Liz has no idea?"

"Not that I know of," I tell him, looking from one mirror to the next for any sign of an approaching squad car. It's getting difficult to keep my voice from trembling.

"Fuck," he says as an almost invisible puff of smoke exits his mouth and takes place just below the ceiling, "that sounds like a lot of effort... Should've just been a door-to-door salesman or something," he grins.

"I don't know," I shrug, "the collar makes people stop when you start talking to them."

"I bet it does," he smirks, smoke billowing from his nose.

"You have anything of Liz's we can listen to?" I ask to break an uneasy silence.

"Like what she recorded? No," he says with a shake of his

head, "I've listened to some online, downloaded tracks here and there, but it's practically impossible to find a hard copy."

"Her band any good?"

"Some of it isn't too bad," he shrugs. "They're nothing new but you can't say they're offensive. Do you *really* have no interest in music?"

"Nothing serious," I laugh. "I've heard my share of records but never had the urge to go out and own one... I've always preferred reading about bands or watching documentaries on them over actually listening to them. Does that really surprise you?"

"Fuck yes," he says, offering me the joint, "you take away fucking and drugs and the only thing that can make you feel the same is a good record. Tell you what; do you have an iPod? Fuck," he realises, "you won't, will you? I would have got you a few tracks. You have a tape deck?" he laughs.

"Afraid not," I smile, bringing smoke inside of me. No bitter taste clings to the back of my throat. The taste is barely noticeable.

"Let's go for a ride," he says, almost sighing as he pulls his seatbelt over.

"Are you sure that's a good idea?"

"Don't worry," he says, "green speeds up my reflexes. We won't go too far; just a couple of blocks so we can tell Liz I was just showing you what this baby can do."

He eases the car forward, stops at a red light and starts drumming his fingers along the edge of the wheel. "But what do you think?" he asks, looking to the CD player so I know what it is he's talking about.

"Yeah," I say, "they sound pretty good."

"Pretty good," he smirks. "They're only one of the most underrated rock'n'roll bands in history. You know people bang on about The Beatles?" The light changes from red to amber. Peter starts the car moving again as he goes on talking. "The Beatles aren't rock'n'roll," he claims. "They were to begin with but as soon as they got the record deal and changed into their pressed suits and became a band who'd go to Buckingham Palace for a nice badge, they sold the fuck out. You can say they *kinda* made up for it with their later records," he continues, "but that wasn't rock'n'roll, that was psychedelic rock, maybe the start of prog."

It's unbelievable but the way he's talking, the conviction he has in every word he has to offer, he has me thinking of how alike he is to Doyle. It's like they could have been close family members or something. I can't take my eyes off him for one minute because of it, can't even close them in case he disappears, so I just stare at him and take long drags on the joint.

"You should look into buying some Slade records," he advises. "There aren't too many of them, they're nearly all good and you know the band will never reform and piss all over the back catalogue. You done with that?"

"Sure," I say, passing him the joint over. I only realise how lightheaded I'm feeling once it's out of my possession.

"Liz," he says, "Liz won't hear a bad word against The Rolling Stones. This is the same Rolling Stones who stopped being important around forty years ago and can now be seen hanging out with One fucking Direction. Sir Mick," he grins, "*Sir* fucking Mick?!"

I start laughing like crazy, I can't help it. I'm doubled over for laughing so hard, sides aching. You shouldn't be able to laugh so hard when you're in this much pain but I am, tears running down my face while I'm struggling to breathe.

"Liz is going to fucking kill me," he laughs, "she's going to say I spiked a priest or something."

I laugh ever harder at that.

"Come on," he chuckles, "help me out, would you? Get control or tell her what you told me."

"I can't," I laugh, "not yet."

<h1 style="text-align:center">18</h1>

Sinclair doesn't seem to have changed at all. It looks the same but I feel it doesn't. There's something different about it all but I can't put quite put my finger on what it is. And my son is walking alongside me. The son I never knew I had until now.

Fifteen years in the world and this is the first time he's ever been with his father. Fifteen years old and I don't even know his name.

He looks normal but he's retarded somehow. In the head or something, I'm not so sure. I can't help but feel the windbreaker he's wearing is a bit of a clue to his condition but it's cold and the rain is falling so it was a good idea for him to put it on. I tell him once, twice how I didn't even know I had a son because he brings up how wrong it was for me, not to have been around all these years, but I don't really hear what it is he's saying exactly. I just have an idea of what he's saying.

He wants to go into the mall so I go in with him. He wants to look around a DVD and record store so I head in behind him. He makes his way like a professional, manoeuvring himself around the other customers, the displays, like he has some kind of radar. I'm struggling to keep him in sight when Eleanor passes me by.

Beautiful Eleanor. She hasn't changed a bit. Not a single wrinkle on her smooth skin and not a single white hair. She smiles at me, mouths some kind of greeting and walks on. I resist the urge to turn and follow her, catch up with my son and stand to the side of him as he examines the back of a DVD that caught his eye. And I just stand there a while, wondering how all of this could have happened and just what the fuck am I going to do next, when I turn to catch up with Eleanor. She's in the next aisle but one, examining a DVD of her own. I stand close to her, just looking at her, in silence. She feels my gaze; turns to me and smiles before putting the DVD back so she can take a step to one side and look at the others on offer.

"I'm sorry," I tell her. "I'm sorry for any pain I ever caused you and I'm sorry if I ever made you feel unloved or unappreciated. I'm sorry for the person I was back then and I wish we could just forget it all and try again because I'd know to be different this time... I'd *want* to be different."

She shrugs the unwanted weight of my confession from her shoulders and tells me how the past is the past and when she looks back on it we were never that great and I didn't make her particularly happy. She tells me all this but I don't hear a sound. That doesn't mean I didn't hear it. Doesn't mean I have no idea at all what she needed to say.

My son appears at my side. I make a quick retreat because I don't want her to know I've got a son and I don't want her to think I'm with somebody else or ever found happiness with anybody else after her. I just rush out of the store, out of the mall and along the cold and wet streets to try and put as much distance between us as possible, hoping doing so will have her remember me and our time together in a different light... Maybe have her willing to give me a second, final chance.

My son takes his dick out, starts spraying my back with warm piss. My quick pace turns into a gentle jog and finally a run but I can't escape him. He chases me, pissing up my back and against the back of my head.

***

I wake up in my bed at the Missionaries, blanket and clothes cast aside. Looking up at the ceiling I run a weak hand through my hair and wonder what it would feel like to find out I had a son. A part of me thinks it could be a good thing, but not the part that knows I don't have the money or the reliability.

There's the taste of stale vomit in my mouth. I don't remember puking but I know it'd be a wise idea to go and check the shared bathroom sooner rather than later.

Peter had taken us both to a fast food restaurant during our little drive because he said it'd be good cover for us if we went back saying we'd stopped for a burger during the time he was supposed to be showing me his car and nothing else. We'd gone inside, sat on stools with ruby red leather cushions and each ordered a double burger with fries and a milkshake. He'd been good enough to pay for both orders. I think he was happy to be alone with me because he asked the questions and I gave him the answers.

"So how long have you been pretending to be a real preacher and what perks have you gotten out of it?"

"Not too long... I lifted the idea from a friend. He was a lot better at it than I was but he died; natural causes. All we ever needed was a little money to one side so we could buy things like smokes or cologne when it became difficult to steal them. But my friend? He'd known a lot of people for a long time. We'd bump into them and they'd hand over bags filled with things we'd need, but that was before the financial crash."

"Didn't you say you'd done time for burglary?"

"And assault. We'd pick a house and watch it a while. When nobody was home, he'd stand outside the front door while I'd break in through the back and let him on in. Any neighbour looked outside to see what the noise was, they'd see a man of the cloth waiting outside, being let in and think nothing more of it. But I was the stupid one. I always forgot to wear a pair of gloves. I guess I thought we'd never get into trouble as long as we kept together."

"He had you forcing entry and never reminded you to wear gloves... Ever think he wanted you to take the fall if the cops turned up?"

"He wasn't like that. He found me with no place to go out in Los Angeles and gave me a place to stay. He showed me how to act around certain people. He tried to show me how to do street preaching but I didn't take it in... I just used to look at him and try to figure out how people could resist making a donation. When he died... When he died I just got up and left with no idea what I was thinking or what to do next."

"This before or after you were incarcerated?"

"After. I was released, found him and he died right in front of me. With no real reason to remain out in LA I made tracks.

Travelled a while, met a girl out in a small town, took a beating because of it and now here I am with you. I'd have missed out on a lot of trouble if Doyle had still been with me."

"Doyle? Wait a minute- I thought your name was Doyle?"

"Nah. Took it from him along with the collar."

"Ha! So what *is* your name?"

By the time we returned to Liz and Terry I was exhausted and practically ready to fall into a deep sleep. I said it was probably down to drinking even though I had been hit by a car not too long ago and Peter backed me up. Liz and Terry believed it easily enough. I'm guessing my eyes weren't too bloodshot from the smoking or the bar wasn't bright enough for them to see but Liz obviously cared which I took as a good sign. Terry was just glad to have his friend back. If I were in his shoes, I'd have been more than happy for the alone time with Liz.

"Did he bore you to death with facts and figures about his car?" she asked me in private with a smile.

"One of my cousins had a car just like it. He didn't look after it half as good as Peter does but it brought back a lot of happy memories."

"That's sweet."

We went to a couple more bars. I got pretty drunk but it was a safe, tired kind of drunk. I didn't reveal my story or tell Liz how I was maybe falling in love with her. At least I don't think I did anyway. Terry got a little friendlier towards me and I'm guessing that was all down to Pete. He got friendlier but he still kept some distance there. If it's because he thinks I'm after Liz then he's right and there's nothing I can do about it.

19

I FOLLOW ONE of the penguins to a room I've never been in before. She was sent to collect me on Abigail's orders so it must be serious. Earlier in the day I'd forced myself out of my room and checked out the shared bathroom, just to be sure I hadn't thrown up in there or left a mess. It looked tidy enough but I guess somebody could have already cleaned it up before me.

The penguin stops at the door, knocks twice and smiles at me. "Here we are," she says.

"Enter," Abigail calls out in response.

The penguin opens the door for me; smiles briefly at Abigail and just stands there keeping the door open for me. I smile at her and stroll on in. The penguin closes the door shut behind me to give Abigail and me a little privacy. The head honcho is sitting behind yet another large desk, counting a handful of twenties. There are neat piles spread out across the table; sets of hundreds I reckon, and a few tin boxes where the cash must be stored. This is a test, no doubt about it, and the idea of failing it by gathering all of that money up before racing out the door sure is a tempting one.

"Mr Doyle," she smiles, "please, sit down."

I sit opposite her, watch her gather up the piles and distribute them amongst the open tins. She takes a set of keys from the table, starts locking the tins. Every key is on the same ring. She does it like she isn't paying me the slightest bit of attention but I know she is keeping an eye on me.

"I'll be with you in a moment," she says, smiling like she's a little embarrassed at my arriving before she's done.

"Take your time," I smile, "I'm in no hurry."

Abigail places the locked tins into drawers on the other side of the desk and closes them. "Now," she says, briefly turning away from me to hang the keys on a small hook on the wall behind her, "let's get down to business, shall we?"

The keys just dangle there in plain sight; tins filled with good money in unlocked drawers to the other side of me. Here the bitch of a snake is, offering me a bite of the apple.

"Barbara has recommended you stay here; a probationary period, of course, so you are entitled to expenses-"

"Expenses?" I deliberately interrupt her, letting her think it surely won't be long until I'm caught with my hand in the jar. *Tins*.

"Expenses," she smiles. "You'll be expected to provide receipts and fill in the right paperwork but I'm sure you'll get the hang of it soon enough. And Tony will be back with us in no time at all," she's happy to reveal, "and I'm sure he'll have plenty of time for you. Don't let Barbara fool you," she says, "she isn't in charge here - Tony is."

"Well," I tell her, getting to my feet, "I look forward to meeting him. Now if you'll excuse me," I add, "I'm off to see if any of the girls need a man's help."

I feel her eyes burning into me as I head for the door. I feel her disappointment at how I didn't make a dive for the keys or tell her there and then how I could sure use a little money. Let the bitch dangle for a while if she wants to be funny. She doesn't have any idea how well I can play it.

20

AT LEAST ONE of the penguins has a car of her own but the Missionaries rent another van and it's Liz who's going out to get the week's shopping. I feel like telling her they're taking advantage, having her pay for her room as well as running all over town whenever they click their fingers, but I keep quiet just so I can head out alone with her. I figure at the very least I'll be able to pick up some deodorant marketed at men so I no longer have to use the one in the pink flower-pattern can that Abigail decided to hand me.

Liz turns to me with a smile and asks, "You ready?"

She's wearing sunglasses despite the fact it's cloudy. In most instances that would annoy me but she looks so adorable in them you have to go on letting her wear them.

"Only for the ride of my life," I say to her with a grin.

"Groovy," she smirks, "but we're going to need some sounds."

She reaches into her jacket pocket and pulls out a CD. Written across the top in what could be her own handwriting is *DRIVING MIX 01.*

"Your own selection?" I ask, watching her feed it into the slot.

"Joint effort," she says, "I put this together with the original guitarist of the band. I think it still holds up pretty well despite the years."

Jangly guitar chords come over the speakers as she starts the engine then puts the car into drive. The sound system sounds nothing as crisp or full as it would in Peter's car.

"Who is this?" I ask her as our journey begins.

"Pulp," she says. "If anybody ever starts going on about the genius of Morrissey's lyrics, just tell them Jarvis Cocker did it better. They won't accept it. They'll just keep going on about Morrissey but you just keep on telling them Cocker was the best at it and in the end they'll take a hike because they can't handle people questioning their supposed raconteur."

"I know The Smiths," I laugh, "I do know *some* things."

"Get you," she laughs, taking a hand from the wheel to reach out for the cigarettes and light up on the dashboard. "You like them or were they another band unable to quite grab you?"

"I don't know," I shrug, accepting a cigarette while delving into a pocket for my Zippo. "A friend used to say how Morrissey had a dry wit."

"A lot of people claim that," she says, "they say he's just being funny or metaphorical and I felt the same for a long time but now I just think he's self-pitying."

It sounds like Jarvis Cocker is serenading Liz over the speakers, telling her how he wants to give her babies. Or maybe he's just telling her how a part of me feels because I can't quite accept it for myself just yet. Everybody has to settle down eventually and Liz is definitely one of the prettiest women I've seen during my time. Even if I hadn't spent so long kept away from the fairer sex and restricted to the company of men I would feel this way.

"We all feel down," she continues, "but there's no real art or depth in Morrissey's words as far as I can tell... Not meaningful, anyway. If you want pain put beautifully," she says, "just listen to what Ian Curtis had to say."

The fact she can see beauty in pain has me wondering where she has been all of my life and praying there's a way to go back in time, make different choices and turn in different directions so I can save myself a lot of trouble and meet her sooner. But if I had the chance, would I really meet her sooner over trying to save Doyle?

"So what do you think," she asks with a smile, "you liking this?"

"It's fun," I say with a casual shrug. "I liked some of the music which Peter played to me the other night."

"Uh-oh," she laughs, "do you remember who it was?"

"Slade," I tell her.

"They have some good songs to their name," she laughs, "but watch out, he does listen to some terrible music. Did he tell you how Slade will never reform because Noddy isn't *a corporate whore*?"

Noddy?

"He mentioned something about them never getting back together."

"If they did," she laughs, "I think he'd have to throw himself off a bridge. You know what I've just realized? You have me and Peter trying to show you the way to good sounds and so far, all we've done is point you towards England, just like anybody else would only they'd be using The Beatles. You ever thought of going there?"

"A friend told me he lived there a while and it wasn't much."

"Probably isn't," she sighs, "but I don't think *we* have anything to write home about any more."

21

Liz says, "That's the last of it," as she places the last bag of groceries into the back of the van and slams the doors shut. "Anything you want to do now?"

I take a pack of cigarettes from my pocket, take two from that and hand her one. I claimed expenses for forty cigarettes and pocketed the change. Abigail had me fill in a contract for the privilege. They wanted a social security number so I made one up on the spot, just like I made up everything else. I'll be long gone before they get wise.

Liz thanks me and lights her cigarette using the cheap disposable lighter she has. I use my Zippo. "How long have we got?" I ask.

"We got all this in record time," she says with a proud smile. "We could easily take a couple of hours for ourselves."

"Okay," I smile, "how about we go for a little walk and stop somewhere for coffee?"

"Coffee's good," she smiles back at me.

We walk around a little while with Liz pointing out the occasional place of interest; the fountain Peter fell into when they were out drinking one night, the bar where Terry lost consciousness while sitting on the toilet, little things like that. But in the end I spot an internet cafe and suggest we go there because the coffee is a good price and the sign says if a computer in a certain zone is available, you use it for free so long as you have a drink in front of you. Liz agrees so we go in, find a free computer in the designated zone and each order a coffee I'm more than happy to pay for.

"Here," I say, moving another empty chair over to the free computer, "you can sit here. Shit," I add, "how are you supposed to login to these things?"

"The waitress will bring a code over with our drinks," Liz explains.

"Ah," I say, "peachy. You know if you can smoke in here?"

"Afraid not," Liz sighs.

"That's moronic," I say, "everybody enjoys a cigarette with their coffee."

"Tell me about it," she laughs.

The waitress brings our coffees over with a two complimentary biscuits and a slip of paper with a six digit code printed across it. As I'm typing it in I look to Liz and say, "Free biscuits? The recession must be over."

Liz jokes, "They'll be bone dry; it's a trick to get you buying more coffee but that just gets you another biscuit. What is it you're wanting to look at, anyway? You have super-important emails to check?"

"No," I say with a shake of the head, "first thing I'm going to do is look up your band."

"Seriously?" she laughs.

"Seriously," I say, entering the name into a search engine. "Peter said you're pretty good."

"Peter knew it would get back to me if he said differently!" she laughs.

The first couple of pages are nothing but photographs of cats standing upright to look out of windows or into running bathtubs. It's disappointing but it's also strange to find out so many people felt the need to share stuff like that.

"Maybe you should have called yourself The Dead Cats," I tell her, "because I can't see many people wanting to share pictures of that."

I change the subject to *Upright Cats band* and hit enter again. We hit paydirt right away.

"Bingo," I tell her.

Articles on the band that appeared in the indie press; reviews of shows on blogs, brief mentions of them when it states they're supporting a bigger act. I move over to images and Liz cringes, temporarily covering her face in shame. "This is so embarrassing," she says.

And there she is, posing with her bandmates in publicity shots or just noticeable on a distant stage in a photograph taken by somebody in the crowd. Different colour streaks to her hair in a lot of the pictures, sexy as hell in all of them.

The easiest thing a girl can do to make a man want her is pick up an instrument.

"You miss this?" I ask her.

"Some of it," she admits.

Liz, my ideal woman without shadow of a doubt. We could settle down and have children. She could return to her music, go solo and tour for a good few months out of every year so we would never tire of each other.

"What about you," she blushes, "will there be any newspaper articles on the good deeds you've done out in LA?"

"Few good deeds go noticed out in LA," I tell her, "but you've given me an idea."

I start the online search for the Missionaries...

She's quiet during the ride back. I light a cigarette for us both and ask, "You feeling okay?"

"Yeah," she says without taking her eyes from the road. It's clear she doesn't mean it.

When I'd eventually found the Missionaries I'd been looking for, I was more than a little happy to see no mention of the church or church endorsement, just the usual garbage of a *charitable organization* being influenced by the *teachings of Christ*. Even the picture of Antony, an image you'd expect of a Sociology teacher in a high school year book, didn't state he was a Father or even a Reverend underneath it. I'd been a little too happy to tell Liz how I now thought we were definitely staying with conmen in sharp suits.

"You sure about that?"

"Well," she says, "you can't say they're not doing something good."

"And lining their own pockets while they're at it," I sigh. "That there is the key reason why I was looking at leaving the church and starting anew."

"Really?" She asks me, "You're thinking of walking away from your responsibilities?"

"I can help people without the collar," I tell her, "and you know something? You of all people should know more than anybody else you don't need a title or a collar to make people in the world feel good, you can do it by simply picking up a guitar. I can do good without oiling the wheels of a corrupt organization. That's all the church really is," I sigh like it pains me to say it, "a big business. They change what was said to suit them and they forget all the meanings. Christ wouldn't recognise one if he came back today."

"So what're you going to do?" she asks.

"Stick around a little while longer," I say, "and pray the good lord sends a sign my way."

22

It's all fun and games in Thingwall's but I can't help but feel a little disappointed at how neither Terry or Peter mention the fact I'm without a dog collar. It's been days since I last sported one. The collar the Missionaries handed me, even the one I took from Doyle, they're both at the bottom of a drawer, buried under donated shirts. But I suppose I should just be happy to see how Liz is feeling a lot better. She's still running around for the Missionaries far too much but there's something different in the way she looks at them when they ask her to run a favour. It's like you can feel her analysing them. Maybe she's just excited by the fact her brother, Iain is coming to visit. They've been speaking on the telephone practically every day so I know he should be turning up sooner rather than later but that doesn't make me any less nervous. If the man is as big a success in business as she says he is, he'll be able to point out a liar like me with his eyes closed and both hands tied behind his back.

I laugh at a punch-line I didn't quite hear and say, "I'm off to take a leak," getting to my feet.

"Look at that," Terry laughs, "needing to go as soon as it's his round."

"I'll get them on the way back, jackass," I laugh before realising I'm not even in a round with him. "Wait a minute," I grin, "I don't even have to get you a drink!"

Not that the money would be coming from my personal savings. The Missionaries seem more than happy to hand the money over so long as you hand in the correct paperwork. The only concern is it might come to a sudden stop once the all-powerful Tony returns from his pilgrimage.

"Worth a try," Terry laughs, "it was worth a try."

I make my way to the bathroom and give a friendly smile to the last barman to have served me like we're good friends or we share a solid bond. He nods his head in mock recognition

76

when really he's doing nothing other than trying to remember if I gave him a good tip and whether he should make a beeline once I'm back at the bar because of it.

I enter the bathroom and stop at a deserted urinal trough to empty my bladder. Behind the closed door of a stall, somebody is sniffing. It's not the kind of sniffing you do to breathe easy, it's the kind you do when you're bringing something white and illegal into your system.

I reckon I've known more drug-users than I have non-users. The country has got to be overrun with them but nobody is willing to open their eyes and see it. One day, a figure in Washington will become aware of this and stand on a platform to announce a vote for him is a vote for the decriminalisation of drugs. Everybody will pounce on the guy; they'll call him to spawn of Satan and they'll say he's a Red out to ruin the free world but come results day he'll have next to 100% of the vote.

I'm about to start pissing when somebody else walks in and right away I can't go anymore. I can feel the piss right at the tip of my dick but it isn't willing to take the jump. I have that problem.

"I'm not disturbing a private conference here, am I?" Terry jokes, stepping up alongside me. A toilet flushes. The stall door opens and the guy with a wrap of coke in his pocket or tucked into one of his socks heads back into the bar without my managing to catch a look at him.

"I got thinking," I shrug. "I forget all about going if I'm distracted."

Terry's pissing already because he would be, wouldn't he?

"Weight of the world on your shoulders?" He says, "You got to drop off as much as you can, buddy."

"I'll try," I tell him. A quick burst of piss shoots free but soon becomes a weak trickle. I silently ask a nameless god not to let it be cancer.

"You seen the new waitress? I'd have to put duct tape up her side to stop me from splitting her in two."

"I'll keep an eye out," I laugh.

"Do that," he says, shaking himself off already. Terry puts his piece away, turns to the sink and starts washing his hands. At long last I start to go to the best of my abilities. Take that, cancer.

"We're thinking of making tracks after one more," Terry says over the sound of the hand dryer, "any suggestions?"

"I'm easy," I tell him, shaking myself off.

"I've heard that," Terry grins, reappearing at my side. "I have something you might be interested in."

Is he doing what I think he's doing?

"No," I grin, "I don't think you have."

"You sure?" he asks, taking a white tablet from his pocket. It's a couple of millimetres thick and one look at it is enough to know you take it dissolved in water. "Co-codamol," he says, "it's a painkiller."

"And?"

"And?" he laughs. "Come on, you're safe with me. Peter let slip when we were having drinks. Just take it," he says, "go on."

I take it, hold it in the palm of my hand and look at it a while before looking back at him.

"You grind it up and you snort it but make sure you only take a little," he says, "and don't make any plans for that day."

"I don't have any idea what you're talking about."

"Sure you don't" he laughs. "Now let's get back to the others and try to decide on where we're going to."

23

I'VE BEEN AWAKE a while. I've dressed but I haven't washed; I've risen but I haven't left my room. Bright sunlight manages to cover every wall despite the fact the curtains are still drawn but there's no way to get me up and about today, I'm just not in the mood.

I light another cigarette. The ashtray on the bedside cabinet is overflowing with cigarette ends even though you're not supposed to smoke indoors here... It's against the rules. I think nothing of it. I don't even start to wonder *where* the ashtray came from, because I sure as hell didn't buy it. Even the acoustic guitar standing in the corner of the room has been accepted. Maybe Liz left it here, maybe it was always here but I simply hadn't noticed.

There's a knock at my door and then it's opening before I've had the chance to tell them it's OK to come in but as soon as I see who it is there's only one thing I can say.

"Doyle," I say in shock.

He's standing there, as big as a house, dressed from head to toe in black. Without the clerical collar he looks a lot like a man from a Western whose motives you'd sure question.

"Lee," he says with a nod and he starts to smile but he doesn't want me to see it so he turns around and softly closes the door behind him. The smile has gone when he turns back to face me but I know he's happy, even if he doesn't want to show it.

"Doyle," I say as he drags a chair over to sit in close to the bed, "you're really here."

"I'm really here," he agrees.

"But in LA-"

"Was in LA," he shrugs, lowering himself down into the chair.

"Doyle," I say, "I thought you were dead!"

"I woke up in a hospital," he says, lighting a cigarette. "They never said anything about bringing me back to life and I don't remember seeing an almighty bright light but that mightn't mean shit."

"What have you been doing?" I ask him, "How did you even manage to find me?"

He shrugs his shoulders, exhales a cloud of blue smoke as slowly as he can to build up a little extra suspense. "I've been here and there," he says. "I crept out of the hospital and headed straight for Saint Claire's but it isn't even there anymore. I tried a couple of churches but not one of them would give me a place to stay, not even for a single night."

"I know that pain," I smile.

"Yeah," he smirks, pausing to pull a little more smoke into his lungs. "I wandered Los Angeles like I didn't even know the place... It's changed and so has everybody there. It was like being in a whole new place so I left and just travelled for a while. In the end," he laughs, "I met up with an old girlfriend, hadn't seen her in years. And she has a son," he says, "*my* son!"

"Doyle," I say with a stupid smile to try and cover my jealousy, "that's great."

"Yeah," he agrees, "it fucking is. I've got the wife, house, kid and dog," he grins. "Even got a job, working security. So I'm living my life," he chuckles, "when I go out to tell somebody to stop loitering and it's an old friend of mine. He told me he'd seen you and where to find you, so here I am."

"This friend," I ask, "was it Owen?"

"It doesn't matter who it was," he says.

"If you reckon," I say, too happy to see him alive to care about what lies he might have told me in another life. "Jesus," I tell him, "you don't know how happy I am to see you right now."

"I feel the same way," he says, dropping a hand onto my foot. "But you know it can't be the same now, right? That we can't see each other as often as we used to, now I've got the wife and a nine to five?"

"Sure," I tell him with a nod as my heart slowly crumbles, "I figured that out as soon as you mentioned your boy."

"I'm glad you understand. But listen," he says, "there's just *one* favour I got to ask of you... One thing to be taken care of for old time's sake. And you know me," he sighs, "I'd do it myself if my circumstances hadn't changed so unexpectedly."

"Right," I say, desperate to prove myself just one more time, "what is it?"

"I need you to kill Cole for me."

I hear him loud and clear but I still say, "What did you just say?" with hopes he'll say something completely different next time around.

"I need you to kill Cole for me," he says for a second time. "Not just because of what he done but because of what he is. You'd even be saving him from a lot of hassle," he laughs. "You know I'd do it myself but I've got my house well and truly in order right now," he reasons. "So do you think you can help me out on this one?"

***

I don't wake up with a sharp intake of air or violently throwing myself into a sitting position. I just open my eyes and accept I was dreaming and now I'm back here in the real world. A single tear runs down from my left eye but I don't wipe it away; I let it run down to the pillow and then I feel the cold patch of cotton under my cheek and do nothing more than hope Doyle is happy.

<h1 style="text-align:center">24</h1>

I drop by Walt's Drugstore to see if he recognises me without the collar; to see what the chances are of him identifying me if he catches me raiding his supplies one day in the near future. He looks up at me, grunts and then looks back down to the newspaper he's reading. It's impossible to tell.

I try convincing myself how I don't care that Liz has been a little off with me the last few days, like I don't care because she's nothing more than a pretty face and it's not like we've gotten intimate, but I do. I can't help but worry. Can't help but want, *need* to know what I've done wrong.

I say goodbye to Walt and walk back onto the street, lighting a cigarette almost immediately. A car horn sounds. I turn to see the hood of a classic Dodge coming to the curb and know right away that it's got to be Peter.

"Lee," he grins, pulling the window down, "how's it hanging?"

"No complaints," I tell him. "What're you up to?"

"Nothing," he says. "You want to come over to my place and have a few drinks, a few laughs? I'll play some good music for you."

"Why not," I say back to him. He pushes the passenger door open for me and I climb inside, rubber burning before I've had the chance to fasten my seatbelt.

"Still no collar? How're they going to get you back to your owners if you're without it?" he jokes.

"Just a little experiment," I tell him. "Terry let slip how you told him about me."

"I'm sorry," he says, "but you've nothing to worry about, Terry won't tell a soul. You know he hates the Missionaries, right? He's taking whatever you get up to under their noses as his own revenge."

"I hope you're right," I sigh. "He gave me a tablet when we were last out."

"See?" Peter laughs. "I told you he was safe. Man," he laughs again, "I didn't even know he was packing. What was it?"

"Painkiller," I tell him, "Co-codamol?"

"Fuck," Peter says, "you have to be careful with that."

"Yeah," I nod, "he said I should only take a little."

"He's right, that stuff can stop the heart... Something like three days after you've taken it, sudden death. I hardly touch it myself."

I'm guessing that's why he didn't offer you any."

"You're probably right. But fuck," he says, "if you've never taken it before, he should have told you not to take it without him being there."

"I haven't taken it anyway."

"I'd advise you not to."

We go on driving with only Peter's choice in music to provide any sound until I decide to speak up again. I ask him, "Have either of you told Liz the truth about me?"

"No," he says with a shake of the head.

"You sure? She's being pretty funny around me. Made it pretty obvious over the last few days she's had better things to do than hang around me."

"Usually," Peter laughs, "I'd say a girl must be on her monthlies but I've known Liz long enough to know it won't be that."

"Then what is it?"

"It's just Liz," he answers. "She's either the coolest cat around or she's a dick and unless you know her properly, you'll think it must be something you've done. I don't know what it is," he shrugs, "whether she's feeling sorry for herself and wishing she was back with her band or whether she has some fucking mental illness she's keeping quiet about but she'll go back to the way she was around you in no time at all. Just don't take it personally."

"If you say so."

"I do," he says, stopping for a red light. "So what were you doing at Walt's?" he asks with a smile. "You still planning the great robbery?"

"You know how it is," I sigh, flicking my cigarette out onto the road, "I can't stay here forever."

"I used to think the same," he says, "but then I realised it's pretty cushy here. I get decent pay for doing next to no work and I can sit back and get high whenever I feel like it. And look at this place," he continues while a number of pedestrians go on making their way to the other side of the road, "there's never going to be any real trouble here. No terrorist on the planet would ever think this would be a good place to detonate a bomb."

"Yeah," I nod, "it's just so boring, isn't it?"

"A little bit of boring can be good," he laughs. "We can't be fucked all of the time, otherwise we wouldn't appreciate it."

"Why not? You know what's going to happen if you're not careful? You're going to end up as deputy manager of a catering business. Could you live like that?" I ask him, "Working a job you hate and having a wife or something in your life to witness your being a failure?"

"You were a lot cheerier when you had a collar," he laughs.

25

I can still hear a couple of guitar solos and repeated verses when I return to my room over at the Missionaries. Peter had played a lot of music and we had drank a lot of beer. The beer was a bad idea because despite what he had told me earlier, I can't shake the bad feeling caused by Liz having an issue with me right now. He'd said she's like that but I can't help but blame myself one moment and hate her the next. A part of me thinks it would be an idea to go right to her room and have it out with her.

I don't have it out with her. I take my shirt off and spread it out on the ground in front of the door to make sure nobody will just come walking straight in and then I take the Co-codamol tablet from its hiding place and just look at it a while.

"Fuck her," I mutter and I start pounding at the Co-codamol with a pen and first it breaks and then it crumbles into smaller and smaller pieces. I concentrate on one section in particular, grinding it down into a fine powder.

How much of this shit is too much? Fuck if I care. I separate what I would consider to be a less-than-reasonable amount of blow and snort it. Feeling a little drunk, a little restless, I pick my shirt back up off the floor and put it on... head back out like a man with nothing to lose. The money in my back pocket is as good as non-existent but I'm sure I still know how to pick a pocket when necessary.

26

THE BAR, LIKE the town it is in, is easy to overlook. I only came in here because I noticed a glowing sign reading BUD ON TAP out from the corner of my eye. And I'm sitting with a bottle of Heineken when the Co-codamol kicks in.

My mind, my thoughts, they're there. It's just that *there* is underneath at least six feet of water.

My body is slow, numb. It's slowly convincing itself it's a statue and not flesh and bone.

My throat feels too big for my neck. My breathing is deep and slow.

Is this what it feels like to die?

I exhale out through my mouth, plan on bringing the bottle to my lips but my arm is too tired to do that right now. It's like I'm stoned for the very first time. My body, my soul, is too far away from me. It doesn't feel good but I don't particularly care.

I take another deep breath, bow my head and somehow wipe a hand over my forehead. The skin is cold and wet.

I take another deep breath and slowly release it, lifting my head and taking in the bar around me. Nobody seems to have even noticed the sorry state I'm in. Some prick a couple of stools away from me is ordering his drink with little more than hand gestures, he's so busy talking into his cellphone. The barman finishes serving him and heads in my direction to do whatever he needs to do and I manage to grab his attention by lifting a hand a couple of inches from the bar. He stops and smiles at me. "What can I get you?" he asks.

"You," I sigh, "you know the Missionaries' number?"

"Missionaries of Charity? It'll be in the phonebook," he says, "we have one out back."

"Do me a favour," I say before inhaling a *lot* of air, "call them, would you? Tell them Lee Doyle needs picking up. Must be food poisoning or something."

"I can do that," he says with a nod, "but you'll have to wait outside. I can't have the risk of you throwing up in here."

It's seems almost impossible to swallow. It seems even harder to take a couple of loose coins from my pocket and drop them in front of him.

"How about you let me wait in here where it's warm?"

"No can do," he replies on gathering up the coins, "consider this payment for the call and my time," he says before turning to disappear out the back.

"Fucker," I mutter, getting to my feet, stool pressed to the back of my thighs in case my legs suddenly give way. I drink a little more beer to try and finish my drink but can't, so I put it down in front of me to light a cigarette because I don't give a fuck whether you can smoke in here or not. And Mr Cellphone is looking at me now, waiting to see if I'll collapse or barf or both.

"You looking at?" I ask him.

"Nothing," he says to avoid trouble, "nothing."

Weak, clumsy legs take me towards the exit. It feels like I'm at sea. A cute brunette, looking to be no older than nineteen, is tuning an acoustic guitar up on the small stage, sitting on a stool with a microphone in front of her. I consider staying just because of her but my legs know better and carry on guiding me out of the place.

It's fucking freezing outside. A clear night sky of blinding stars and a full moon. My throat, the muscles in my neck do a brief dance that has me ready to throw my guts out all over the floor but nothing happens.

"Jesus," I sigh because that's all I have the strength to do, "Jesus."

Back against the wall, I slowly bend my knees and ease myself down into a sitting position. Even the sidewalk is cold as ice.

"Come on, Liz," I mutter as night air strips my skin to the bone, "hurry your ass on over here."

27

MY THROAT CONTINUES to swell. It's numb but I know it's swelling because my neck feels ready to burst. And the cold is unbearable. It drives fingers of ice to my heart and tears me apart.

I can hear the pretty girl singing as she plays her guitar. She serenades angels to come take me away.

Car lights appear at the corner and head towards me. My heart lifts but I realise it's an old pickup truck and not Liz. Not even one of the penguins. Just some Joe out to tow a car or something.

Lights bathe over me, consume me, crawl the wall at my back as the van comes to a stop and sits there with the engine running like the driver has come to watch me die. I'd light a cigarette if my hands weren't dead from the cold.

The driver of the pickup truck sounds the horn and hops out of the vehicle. He's wearing beaten cowboy boots with faded blue jeans and a flannel shirt open over a Limp Bizkit t-shirt. Man's around forty and something about him is familiar, it's just I'm having difficulty remembering why.

"Doyle," he says, "boy, do you look like shit."

I wonder whether he has me mistaken for the *real* Doyle. Try to figure out whether I *am* the real Doyle. I'm just too fucked to really think about anything for too long and the cold is a real distraction.

"Doyle," he says, coming closer and kicking at the heel of my left shoe with the toe of his right boot. There's a toothpick hanging from his lips. I didn't think anybody did that in real life. "Shit," he says, "you are in a bad way."

"You're the gardener," I say weakly. Once I've spoken the words my mind becomes a little clearer where he's concerned. I've seen him a couple of times around the Missionaries' building, washing the windows and tending the few plants on show. As a matter of fact he tends to do pretty much every odd-job they must see as being too manly for Liz to take care of.

Liz. Bitch didn't even come pick me up herself.

"You stand?" he asks.

"Sure," I say and I struggle to get myself up into a crouching position. I'm about to tumble back onto my ass but the gardener or whatever his title happens to be catches a hold of me, lifts me with a hand under each armpit and guides me towards his ride.

"Easy," he says, opening the passenger door for me, "come on now."

He guides me into the seat, closes the door behind me and walks in front of the truck to get to his side. It's a hell of a lot warmer in here than it is out on the street but he opens the door and cold air rushes in at me. It's gone the moment he slams his door shut. He looks at me and asks, "You think you're going to hurl?"

There's a foam gun hanging from the rear view mirror with I DON'T CALL THE COPS written over it in bold red letters. There's a sticker across the dashboard with BELIEVE IN JESUS AND JESUS WILL BELIEVE IN YOU written across that.

"No," I tell him, "I just need to get some sleep."

I remember how Peter had told me Co-codamol can stop your heart some three days after you've taken it and wonder if I've gone and taken far too much. I wonder if the man beside me will hide my body if I die on the ride back... Wonder if he'll use my skin for a lampshade or eat me or fuck me or use me for target practice. All he has to do is say I wasn't there. Nobody will spend too long looking for me if I disappear.

"You sure?"

"I'm sure," I answer and I know I'm not going to barf in his truck because if I did he would no doubt fuck my mouth with whatever hand-cannon he has concealed on him.

"Let's go," he says.

Poorly treated gears moan as he gets the truck ready and then we're moving along. Surprisingly, it's no bad feeling. It has me suspecting I'm about to be rocked to sleep and if I never wake up, what difference would it really make?

"What do you think of this place?" he asks. I'd been hoping for a journey back in silence, having the radio on at the most, but the guy clearly has other plans. He figures if he's giving me a ride then I can at least give him some conversation.

"Quiet," I tell him.

"Sure is. You came from out in Los Angeles, didn't you?"

"I guess."

"What's it like out there?" He asks me, "Gang trouble?"

"I can't remember seeing any."

"Seriously? No fighting over drugs or any of that?"

I take a deep breath, slowly release it. My eyelids are heavy and it's getting harder to swallow but I keep going regardless. "Heard about drug pushers near where I was living but didn't see any of them for myself."

"Drugs are everywhere," he says.

"Yeah," I nod, "you can say that again."

"That's the coons for you. When I was young," he says real loud, "man from the church said blacks were black because God had punished them but you wouldn't get away with saying that now. And who're we to suddenly erase God's judgement?"

"You were really told that?"

"Sure was," he says, "God punished them and sent them out to Africa where they bred with gorillas or monkeys. How else can you explain how they look and behave?"

"You," I ask in growing disbelief, "were told that by the church?"

"You mean you wasn't?"

"No!"

"You see?" he asks a little too excitedly. "*That* is exactly what I'm talking about! No wonder this country is in the sorry mess it's in right now! Church can't teach the truth and the government is handing everything over to the Muslims on a plate! Whatever happened to Rhea? That man would have got my vote. That man would have really stirred things up and made a fine president."

28

Sitting beside me on the smoker's bench, Doyle scratches at his throat as if to remind me of the collar I lifted from him. "Look at the state you've gotten yourself into," he grins, finally lighting a cigarette of his own. "Prescription painkillers," he says as if he disagrees with them.

"The stuff I saw you swallow," I sigh, blowing smoke from the side of my mouth. "And the downers you used to have after Olanzapine?"

"Not a painkiller," he says, "*never* a painkiller."

"I suppose not. But what have you been up to?" I ask.

"Very little," he says. "You taken care of that thing for me?"

"What *thing*?"

"You know," he says, "Cole."

"No," I say, shaking my head. "I haven't had the time."

"Make it," he says, "it needs to be done."

The door to the Missionaries opens and Eleanor comes walking out looking prettier than I ever remembered. My heart lifts at the sight of her beauty. Muscles in my legs prepare to lift me, to guide me to her.

"Here comes my ride," Doyle says, getting to his feet before me. "It was nice to see you."

"Wait a minute," I ask him in horror, "you're with Eleanor? Jesus! You can't do that, I fucking love her!"

"What?" He asks me, "You think she was going to hang around forever? Sinclair and her people were bound to move on."

***

I wake up feeling like shit. It's not enough I haven't been able to eat, have barely had the energy to get up out of bed and stumble to the toilet, having to tell one visiting penguin after another how it's all something I ate or a bug, I had to dream of losing

Eleanor and have my heart sliced with a cutthroat razor because of it. Dreaming of Eleanor or seeing or hearing something that reminds me of her only leaves me feeling blue for a good few days. I have to picture *what might have beens* and picture sunny events that never happened.

This all happens no matter how many times I remind myself how we didn't always quite fit, even if nostalgia tries to convince me otherwise.

We had our arguments like couples do. Always about something that didn't really matter but her response was to try and have it out whereas I always went for the silent treatment. I'd listen to her for a while as she tried to get her point across with an increasing amount of anger and I'd just be there, keeping my words and my hatred locked up inside of me until I'd offer her a single sentence or less regarding the last point she had made. She hated that silence, she really did. Upset her some and then a little more. And I don't know for sure where the silence in me had come from. I hardly spoke around my uncle and that was down to fear. I was scared that saying the wrong thing would have him kick me out of the house or worse. And he was a big man. If he had ever gone for me like he used to my mother, I'd probably have had to sit back and take it. Take a beating and maybe you'll still have a roof over your head. Take a beating and try fighting back and you're bleeding out on the streets once it's finally over.

Or maybe I was scared of having something in common with Uncle Nick.

That man could get his back up over nothing and he wouldn't let it drop. I'd give him the silent treatment but he'd still be coming back into the room every couple of minutes if I hadn't been smart enough to get out of there already. He'd charge back in and start yelling about something, like it'd been going through his mind over and over again until it just drove him crazy- his figuring where you would have taken the argument, that is. In, out, in, out and sometimes it would end with the back of an open hand or a push to the face... Anything that would end with you on your ass. Maybe that's how I would have been if I didn't swallow my anger. Let it burn at my insides to keep others from it, I don't know. I've never really had it in me to just let myself go. I've never wanted to be that kind of person.

29

And just like Christ I rise on the third day.

I'm still not feeling so hot but I make myself get up and out of my bed. The sheets are cold or damp with sweat and just standing has me feeling like I'm going to hurl, has my body begging me to just get back under the covers, but I don't. I take my time moving around the room, stopping to notice how Doyle's off-white collar is sitting on top of the dresser and fail to remember putting it there myself.

"You haunting me now, Doyle?"

Long ago, before his corpse was handed over to medical students or tossed into an unmarked grave, Doyle admitted how he'd been meaning to ask me to kill Cole at one point. He'd resisted. If his spirit was hanging around due to a change of plan, my old bed partner must have done something really bad.

"Tell you what, if you're here make me feel a little better... Use your spirit powers to stop me feeling this way."

The shitty feeling doesn't budge. I shrug, slip into a pair of jeans and shirt that feel a little greasy and step out of my room with something resembling a clear head for the first time in days. The carpet beneath my feet is like wire but I don't go back for socks. I make my way down the stairs and out back, cold paving stones at the soles of my feet. There's nobody out here. Nobody but a statue of Christ near the smoker's bench. I look him in the eye and say, "Let's call it a draw," before sitting my ass down and lighting up. Even the bench feels colder than it should. I ignore it, pull smoke inside of my lungs and tell myself it's all just part of the funk I'm still to shake free of. Smoking isn't so fun when you get nothing other than a realisation it is now *just a habit*. It's even worse when the smoke seems too heavy, like tar, and it feels like your chest is about to explode because of it. I sigh, stub the cigarette out on the bench and toss it away with ideas of heading back inside where it's warm.

94

Fucking Liz comes walking on out with her cigarettes in one hand and a light in the other. She spots me, smiles and heads over with a spring in her step. Just getting the idea that everything is cool between us is enough to have me extract another cigarette from my own pack and light up. I'm weak like that.

"He's risen," she jokes, dropping down beside me. "Some of them were saying you'd never pull through but I had faith in you. I always will."

"It was pretty close for a while," I tell her with a grin. "I saw bright lights and heard heavenly harps but I turned my back on it all because I was scared I'd never see you again."

"Aw," she says on taking my elbow and placing her cheek down on my shoulder, "what would I do without you?"

I don't know if we're both joking or trying to let one another know how we really feel. All I know for certain is the way we're positioned right now is causing a little excitement down the front of my pants and I probably shouldn't try getting to my feet for a little while because of it. I give her one of my nicest smiles- a smile that says I know *exactly* what we're doing right now - and tell her, "You'll never have to find out."

"Sweet," she says back to me, lighting a cigarette of her own. "So will you be accompanying me to the ball tonight?"

"What ball?"

"We've a soup kitchen on," she says like it's no big deal and I figure that to her, it isn't. She just wants me there as extra security, another pair of strong arms to prevent men that are out of luck from trying to get lucky with her whether she likes it or not.

"Oh," I reply, "right. Sure, I'll come lend a hand."

"That's great," she smiles, "we're going for drinks straight after and then we're ending up at Peter's place. Well," she adds, "it's actually his uncle's but he's looking after the place for the next week and a half."

The time at the soup kitchen drags by because I'm still not feeling all too hot. I stand in the corner instead of sitting with Terry and Peter; make out I'm watching over things. One of the penguins- Helen, I think- is all smiles and soft eyes to the poor souls in search of warmth. Liz looks over at me from time to time and smiles but I only have the energy to return half of one back to her and I hope she thinks I'm being funny because of how she was being with me just a small number of days ago.

We pack up, leave and all meet up again at Thingwall's. In the time we were alone, Liz had been trying a little harder to make some good feeling between us. I tried my best to have her feel like everything was just solid gold because she isn't the kind of girl you can stay mad at. It's a struggle to drink and I have to keep playing catch-up with the others but the beer eventually does its job and makes me feel a little better... A little lighter. Before closing time, Peter suggests we make tracks to his uncle's place.

30

It reminds me of one of those big plantation houses found down south but a lot smaller... Reduced in size to accommodate the average man. What I'm saying is if Tryfords was one of those towns where big stars relocate for a while, they would live in a house like this. The mailbox (with COOK stencilled across the side) at the end of the drive looks like it was dropped there by accident.

"This is a nice place," I say, lighting a cigarette. "What does your uncle do for a living?"

"I don't know," Peter shrugs like it isn't important. "He sells stuff for the bank or something."

The moment we step inside, we know Peter has been here for a couple of days already. Open crates and boxes holding records on both CD and vinyl have been left in the middle of the floor, various releases spread out around them. There's also the noticeable smell of pot in the air. Peter says, "Take a seat, I'll go get something from the drinks cabinet."

"Something classy," Terry calls after him with a smirk, "something vintage."

The nearest couch looks like it has a white velvet cover or something just as fragile. The carpeting on the floor around us is pearl. I lower myself down into a sitting position with the greatest of care and look for an ashtray. Terry just drops himself down onto the nearest recliner and lights a cigarette like he doesn't have a care. "Check out the TV," he says. It's the biggest I have ever seen and the screen curves a little. "Peter," he yells, "your uncle have cable or what?"

"He has a couple of different things," Peter calls back from wherever. "But screw the TV and put some music on, would you?"

"Anything but Slade," Liz says with a grin and then she looks over to me as if she's looking for my approval. I just give her a quick smile before looking away, watching Terry as he gets to his feet and takes to rummaging through the vinyl records.

"You think vinyl will ever stop selling?" I ask.

"I don't know," he says, "probably. Everything that's good is digital already."

"Vinyl sales still make up quite a lot of the numbers," Liz says.

Terry goes on looking through the records and says, "It's just snobbery," without looking back at her.

"Right," she laughs, lighting a cigarette, "says the man who made a beeline to the vinyl!"

"Just seeing if he had anything rare," Terry explains and to prove a point, he pushes the crate aside and turns his attention to the nearest CD collection.

"Drinks for the guests," Peter happily announces on his return, a meal tray with four glasses of an as yet unknown alcohol mixed with coke and four shot glasses of something brown in his possession. He doesn't mention the fact we're all smoking despite the fact there isn't a single ashtray in sight. "Well," he says to me, "are you ready to be fully indoctrinated into the world of music?"

"I *know* music," I laugh, "there are even records I've enjoyed-it's just I've never felt the need to own a lot of them or make such a big deal over them!" It's a statement I'm tiring of giving.

"He's never heard a record he wanted to make a big song and dance about," Terry says with a proud smile.

"That's good," Peter says approvingly, "I like that one. But come on," he adds, "what're we starting with here?"

"I'm looking," Terry says, "I'm looking. I'm feeling a little noisy," he adds, "where's all your grunge?"

"Sold it," Peter says, placing the meal tray down on the coffee table. I lean forward to claim a glass and drop a little dead ash onto the table in the process. Peter doesn't bat an eyelid so I figure I've found the best place for my cigarette to hover.

"You sold it?" Terry gasps in horror. "What the fuck were you thinking?"

"I don't know," Peter smirks, lowering himself into a chair, "I guess I was thinking I'm not thirteen anymore and the whole grunge scene was all fake and irrelevant and most of the biggest names of the day were just boring."

"Sure," Terry sighs, "you could say the same fucking thing about punk-rock."

"Could not," Liz replies. "Look at England alone after the punk movement; post-punk, underground, goth, indie/alternative. A lot of good stuff followed punk-rock. It wasn't as big but it was arguably better."

"And that's punk-rock for the win," Peter says to Liz with a smile.

"Right," Terry says as he continues to thumb his way through Peter's record collection. "Punk was fantastic- that's why it stopped Paul McCartney and Wings getting to the top of the British charts with Mull Of Kintyre in its prime. Oh wait,"he says sarcastically, "it fucking didn't!"

"Right," Peter laughs.

"And what's this?" Terry asks, lifting a CD from the rest and holding it up as if to prove a point. "Like it isn't bad enough having Alice Cooper's *Welcome To My Nightmare* on vinyl- you had to have it re-mastered."

"What are you on about?" Peter smirks, getting to his feet and taking the record from Terry's possession. "Cooper always was and always will be cooler than most of the jokers you believe in. Jokers," he adds, "who all tend to fall into the same genres."

As if to prove a point, he walks over to the stereo and puts the record on.

31

ON HER HANDS and knees, she says it feels amazing.

We'd all carried on drinking and smoking. The mess we mad e- a drink spilled here, ash dropped there - went from being a big part in the jokes we made against one another to not being noticed anymore. Jokes were made about Peter's uncle coming home early and finding us there, ruining his perfect home, and we all laughed but from time to time I did find myself worrying about what would happen to us if it went and happened. I pictured his uncle much like I picture my own; a giant of a man who'd snatch the bravery from inside your heart and step on it. I got the fear a couple of times because of that; cleared my head by standing outside and on my own for a while, looking up at the full moon and thin wisps of cloud up in the night sky. After that, I made a point of only focusing on what I had around me to be happy about.

I can't remember how it happened but we got to talking about what songs we would have played at our respective funerals. I said, figuring I would be cremated instead of buried, it would have to be David Bowie's *Slow Burn*. The others applauded that. Liz made a point of saying I clearly knew some good music after all. Peter said he would have Slade's *How Does It Feel?* and Terry went for Creedence Clearwater Revival's *Someday Never Comes*, which Peter joked was too good a song choice for him to have. Liz thought about it the longest before finally settling on Elvis Costello's *I Can't Stand Up For Falling Down*. Peter found her song choice hysterical but Liz said it wasn't just to raise a smile but because it had been the first song she had learned how to play on the bass.

We all agreed to write down our own copy of the songs, just in case one of us was hit by a bus the following day but we never got around to writing them out. We were too busy laughing and joking, too busy being alive, to think about our own mortality for too long. In the end, it came down to me and Liz. Terry had long fallen asleep; Peter was awake but struggling. He was slumped down low in his chair, eyes red and glassy. Liz had suggested the two of us head back to the Missionaries.

"Don't be stupid," Peter had said, "there's plenty of room for you to put your head down here."

"Some other time," Liz had told him. And I was glad one of us had decided we were leaving because I'd been worrying about Peter's uncle returning home unexpectedly again.

"At least let me call you a cab," Peter had said, struggling to get back up and onto his feet.

"Don't be silly," she said, "we'll catch one out on the street."

It had gotten a lot colder; we all felt it as soon as we were standing at the open door. Peter took a couple of steps back to try to escape it and said, "Are you sure you're leaving?" but he was already preparing to close the door behind us, desperate to force the cold back outside.

"We'll be fine," Liz said, "me and the street preacher here are hard as nails."

I hugged Peter goodbye and caught up with Liz. For a while the only thing we could find to talk about was just how cold it was. I noticed a couple of cabs but didn't point them out until they had gone by and wouldn't have turned around even if we had begged them to. I think Liz was doing the same. So we walked on, the deaf house coming into sight long before we'd started a heated discussion over god knows what. We both seemed to be pretty defensive; both certain it was the other making the attack. And then we walked into the grounds of the deaf centre, both following the other without bothering to ask *why* we were headed there. A couple of the lights were on. I wondered if it would be Bobby or Martin or both of them up there but I can't tell you why. We didn't see either one of them looking out, trying to work out what we were doing back there already. Didn't see them looking out and seeing we're all just moths heading for various flames.

"The problem with you," I said as we stopped under a light and looked to one another, actors in a play sharing the spotlight, "is you're an emotional cripple."

Even as I said it I had no fucking idea why I was saying it. How I'd even managed to throw the accusation out at her like that. And somehow I can't remember for the life of me what she had replied but then we kissed. It was a long, meaningful kiss. She smiled at me when we separated and lowered her eyes, all bashful-like. I apologised despite my not being sorry. I just felt it was what you do in such a situation because I'd seen it done like that in hundreds of movies and TV shows.

"Don't be," she said, "it was nice," and she leaned forward and kissed me, much softer this time. We linked hands and continued the walk back to the Missionaries. Every once and a while I'd twist my upper body a little so I could kiss her again, never once breaking our stride. I did it to try and stop her from regretting what had happened... I wanted her to feel that this was what she really wanted. We hardly said a word but it didn't matter. We didn't quit holding hands until we were in sight of the place acting as our temporary lodgings. Liz made out she pulled her hand free to take the key from her pocket and I tried to pretend that was the reason but deep down, we both knew different.

"Be quiet," she said in a whisper, "it's against the rules to come or go this late."

She led the way inside and I let her close the door behind us. I could hear the blood pumping through my veins. I could hear the ticking of the grandfather clock in one of the rooms upstairs. I listened more than anything for the sound of Abigail taking quick steps to the light switch, desperate to blind us and catch us in the act at the same time.

"Come on," Liz said, "we're not out of the woods yet."

And I ended up in her room, on her bed. Liz said, "Switch the lamp on, would you?" and I reached out for a switch but Liz rushed forward and took a hold of my wrist before I could flick it. "Not that," she said, struggling not to laugh, struggling even more to remain quiet, "that's the panic button!"

"Panic button? Are you serious?"

"You don't have one in your own room?"

"I don't think so."

"Must only be in rooms for women," she said. "It's because of the number of unknown men we have staying here. You'd have pressed that," she told me, "and a local security firm would have been rushing in here with their guns out long before the cops had a chance to hear it."

We'd laughed in near silence. She'd poured her heart out to me and I had poured something out that was near enough my own but not quite. Confessions of losing faith. Declarations of having never felt this way before.

We'd started to fuck. Again, it was all so near silent. I'd long pegged her as being a girl who'd have sung like Liza Minnelli with every thrust but she kept quiet. That didn't mean she wasn't enjoying it. And on her hands and knees she had said it felt amazing.

Amazing.

Her adjective of choice.

32

PETER TURNS TO me as Terry makes his way to the toilets and says, "There's no way he's gone for more than a couple of weeks."

Three weeks earlier, Terry had turned up at Thingwall's full of life and got himself an orange juice instead of a beer. Was even chewing the gum that releases nicotine instead of smoking. He'd said, "I nearly fucking overdosed over the weekend! I was out with Mike and Dave -you know Dave, right? - and we were hitting it pretty fucking hard. We ended up in O'Langshaw's because Dave has a thing for one of the barmaids there and I was just coming out of the toilet when my fucking eyes went. It was like I was watching a movie on widescreen. Honest to god, black bars at the top and bottom of my vision. Then I could see my feet but it was like I was walking up a wall instead of along the ground.

"I collapsed," he said, "Dave and Mike had to carry me out of there. They had to keep me talking all through the night but I can't remember any of it. They said I was puking my guts up, lips blue and everything. I'm telling you," he said, "I'm knocking all of that shit on the head."

We thought it wouldn't last but Terry was out to prove us all wrong. He was running twice a day and hitting the gym three times a week. He wasn't smoking, wasn't drinking, wasn't doing anything that your average person does for a good time. Then, without warning, he told us he was moving on. He had set himself the target of writing the great American novel but he said he had to see the country to do that properly.

Unbelievably, the bank had given him a loan to go walkabout. Liz had missed most of this because she had taken a dislike with Terry for some reason. What she knew is what I told her and even then she didn't seem too interested. She hadn't even replied to the message he sent her about his leaving party.

"What makes you say that?"

"This new way of life he has," Peter says, "it won't last. The first hostel with some backpacking babe he crashes at will have him go back to normal. He'll be back at home in a couple of weeks, engaged or divorced."

"I don't know," I say, "he's out with us right now on his own leaving night and all and he hasn't touched anything but juice or cola."

"I've been tempted to take a sniff at his drinks," Peter grins, lifting his own bottle of beer from the table. "He seems a little too excited for somebody without drink. If it isn't vodka," he says, "he'll have a secret little stash of speed on him."

"They say you should write what you know," I laugh.

"Someone told me Philip K. Dick was the same," he says, drinking a little beer. "They said he was known for taking stuff like that while he was writing. No idea how true it is myself, I've never looked into it."

"Lemmy was supposed to really like the stuff when he was a little younger."

"Look at you," Peter jokes, "trying to pretend you know about music."

"I know I prefer him to Ozzy."

"Wise choice," he laughs. "But in other news," he asks, "how're you and Liz getting on? You two official?"

"I don't know," I sigh, "we haven't really talked about it and we're still being real careful. The Missionaries would toss us out if they knew what we were getting up to under their roof."

"But you're happy?"

"Yeah," I smile, "I'm happy. I like being around her."

"Good. It's a shame you couldn't get her to come out tonight. I know Terry is acting like he hasn't noticed but he'll be a little upset at how she's being with him."

"Yeah," I nod. "Do you have any idea what it's about?"

"I doubt Liz even knows what it's about. No offence."

33

I'm enjoying my own company out on the smoker's bench when he comes through the door. The man looks at me for a moment, then looks around to be sure there is nobody else around as he takes a pack of Marlboro's from his breast pocket. The suit he's wearing looks reasonably expensive. It makes the brace he has on his right leg all the more noticeable. The shoe on the left foot is narrow and sleek, the one on the right looks like it could belong to Herman Munster. He takes his time lighting his cigarette, using a Zippo lighter that produces a narrow, sharp blue flame and then he comes heading in my direction, eyes locked on me.

"Doyle," he asks on getting closer, "Mr Lee Doyle?"

"Who are you?"

He takes a leather wallet from his pocket, flashes it without even opening it and then it's back out of sight. "Jake Maypole," he says, "*detective*. Could I have a moment of your time, Mr Doyle?"

It's all high walls and shrubbery out here, no chance of me climbing out in a hurry. But then there's his leg and how it counts against him. I could shove him to the ground and run through the building and out onto the street long before he's gotten to his feet and taken to hobbling after me. I think better of it.

"Sure," I nod. "What's all this about?"

"Well," he says, sitting himself down beside me, "there have been a number of home burglaries out in Los Angeles-"

I start wondering what the chances are of him carrying a gun. Start wondering if he'll fire a warning shot into the air or aim for one of my legs as I'm rushing to the exit. Most likely he'll fire a shot at my knee, taking some sick pleasure in seeing I spend the rest of my days like him.

"We've had no leads until now," he says. "A sweet old girl

walked in and saw our suspect in her bedroom, sniffing at one of her sex toys."

"Excuse me?"

"The man was sniffing at one of her sex toys," he says. "Quite an expensive model; seventeen inches long and something like four and a half inches thick. She says you have to keep a stick of butter on the bedside table at all times because of it."

I can't believe I'm hearing this. I don't know what to say or what he could possibly say next but then he's laughing.

"I'm sorry," he says, "but I can't do this any longer!"

Liz comes rushing out the door, smiling the biggest smile I have ever seen and laughing like she's just heard the funniest joke of all time. "You should have seen your face!" She laughs. "Lee, it was a picture!"

The supposed detective offers me his hand. "Name's Iain," he says, "it's a pleasure to meet you."

"Iain," I chuckle, "the twin, right?"

"I prefer to see myself as the older brother," he grins.

34

Iain waits until the waitress has finished taking our orders before revealing why he always orders shrimp when eating out at a Chinese restaurant.

"You got the chicken and you got the beef," he says, "but it could be anything. Friend of mine back at college worked in a Chinese restaurant much nicer than this one and he said it'd surprise you how many times they'd have dog or horse or something hanging up in the back. When I look at my meal," he says, "I'll *know* I have the meat I ordered. You two could have anything."

"I know what beef tastes like."

"Do you?" he smirks.

A waiter comes over to our table with a bottle of red Iain had requested. He pours a small amount of it into a glass for Iain to try, just like in the movies. Iain thanks him, sniffs at the drink and then swills it around the inside of his glass a little. Tiffany used to do the exact same thing and every time, I used to wonder what would happen if she had said the wine wasn't good enough. I find myself hoping Iain will say something along those lines, just so I'll finally get an answer.

"That's good," he says after drinking a little, "it's more than drinkable. Fill them up, would you?"

The waiter gives him a polite nod and a smile, topping up Iain's glass before starting on both Liz's and my own.

"How many jokes have you heard about wine and Christ's blood?" Iain asks me.

"All of them," I smirk.

"I could believe that. I was thinking of making one but thought you'd be long bored of them."

"Thanks for the consideration," I laugh.

The waiter finishes with our glasses and leaves us alone. Iain examines his wine in the light and sighs. "This is something else

I don't get," he admits. "Wines. I understand how the cheaper wines can be a bit of a gamble because I've had my share, but there are some good wines available priced a couple of hundred apart and it's not like you can taste any real difference. You ask me," he says, "any wine priced somewhere along the middle is good enough. The higher the price, the bigger the fool they're making out of you. I mean," he laughs, "what is it- Lionel Richie serenades the grapes of the more expensive wines?"

"I tried Buckfast out on the road," Liz adds with a smirk. "I don't get how anybody could drink that without mixing it."

"You gave me a bottle of it one Christmas," Iain smiles back at her, "I think it's safe to say that it's still in my cellar."

"You have a wine cellar?"

"Came with the house," Iain chuckles. "Once I bought the house, I realised I'd always have to be stocked up on wine."

"Your line of work is that good?"

"Oh," he says, "you wouldn't believe it! Take something like a lock for example," he says, "the kind you'll find on a front door. You can pick one up for a couple of bucks but a little further along, you see one going for- I don't know- let's say eighty bucks. You're not going to spend eighty bucks on a lock but would you feel comfortable picking up the cheapest one after seeing the price difference? No, you wouldn't. You'd maybe splash out and get one for around twenty, then buy a security chain for a bit of extra comfort but again, you don't buy the cheapest chain. That's just one person," he says, "so imagine all the people in the construction business or are moving home that come by within the space of a week. That is a lot of money," he brags, "and I sell a lot more than locks."

"So locks are your number one seller?"

"Locks and safes," he says. "A lot more people are buying safes nowadays," he explains, "because they don't want *all* of their money in a bank but nobody wants to just hide their hard-earned under the bed or a loose floorboard these days, so they buy a safe. As soon as they're looking at safes, they're looking to the ones that have more than the one lock mechanism and, wouldn't you know it, *that* safe next to it is fireproof!"

"You ever see someone spending a lot of money and tell them they could get a cheaper safe or lock which is almost as good?"

"Absolutely not," he says, "firstly, because I have no idea what it is they're protecting, secondly because it's my job to sell peace of mind. If I start undermining the customer's choice, they won't know what brand or name to trust."

"I'm just nipping to the bathroom," Liz says on getting to her feet.

"Take a peek in the kitchen on your way there," Iain jokes, "see if they've coaxed in a stray dog from the alley yet. You must understand a little of what I'm saying," he says to me, "what with your profession? What if a woman who had always attended your services turns around one day and says, I don't know, she's going to give the Indian elephant a try for a change?"

"I don't know," I laugh, "I don't know how I'd react to that at all."

Iain glances over my shoulder to check Liz is in the bathroom before leaning closer to me and saying, "She likes you. You do know that, don't you?"

"I'd like to think so," I grin, "we're good friends."

"Well," Iain says, "and I hope you don't mind my saying this, but I've noticed something between the two of you. How highly she thinks of you was my first clue and the second was seeing how you act around one another. You bounce off each other," he smiles, "it's like you positively feed one another."

"I'll admit," I smile, "I am fond of her..."

"You know what I think? I think it would be an injustice if you two didn't help one another out, if you two weren't there for one another, because it looks to me like that's the reason why you were brought together. She tells me you're doubting how much good there is in the world and here she is, giving you all you need. And her," he sighs, "she's like a different person around you. No," he says, "not a different person, just her at her best. You two come together and everything in your world is right. I think it would be good karma for me to just keep you two close to one another," he grins.

"I don't know," I smile weakly. "Maybe we were just looking

for something and we're hoping we've found it. Problem is," I sigh, "that doesn't mean we have."

"No," he says like he knows it all, like he's examined every blueprint and design in great detail, "I know what I see the very moment I see it. Hearing her talk about you has put my mind at rest," he admits. "That apparent religious outfit she's with? They've got bad news written all over them in permanent marker and you've come down and rescued her from it. A girl like her," he says, "they'd throw in front of the media the second people find out they're doing shady deals and secret handshakes and the worst thing is that I'd be paying them for the privilege- the money I've been handing over to them because I've wanted to keep her away from the open road and all the badness it has to offer her!

"I'd sleep easy knowing you were near her and I think you would too."

3 5

WE CLAMBER INSIDE a cab alongside one another, all laughing and joking. It's been a good night. I watch Iain and Liz as they both make fun of one another but it's all innocence and joy, not a drop of spite between them. And it continues like this until Iain leans in close to the driver and says, "Just take the next right and stop at the corner for one second, would you?"

The driver does as is asked of him, stops the car on Waimanalo Drive.

"Come on," Iain laughs, "hop out here for one minute, would you?"

Liz looks to me and starts laughing, unsure as to whether we should follow. A cold wind is blowing and it's bringing rain down with it.

"Come on," Iain laughs, "come on."

We follow him out onto the street. Iain points to a large store that has stood empty for a while. Shutters covered with brightly coloured slogans and names, a wide rectangle long bleached by the sun where the store's identity was once displayed proudly.

"Well," Iain asks, "what do you think?"

"What do I think about *what*?" Liz asks.

"This place," Iain says, taking carefully measured steps towards the abandoned building. "Behold, my newest palace," he says laying an open hand against the shutter, "behold my embassy on this sacred soil."

"Are you saying what I think you're saying?" Liz excitedly asks. "Are you moving here?"

"Yes and no," he smiles. "I purchased the building," he shrugs, "I own it. I have workmen starting on it in the next few days so it'll be ready to open within the month. And I'm going to have a big recruitment drive," he goes on, "but I think I'm looking at my store manager and deputy manager right now.

"Then there's the two bedroom apartment facing it from

right across the street," he says, "quite a nice place, next to no work needs to be done there at all and I'll gladly pay to have it furnished. The only real work needing doing is to make it exactly how you want it."

Liz looks at me and starts laughing; turns to Iain and excitedly jumps nearer to him like a bunny. "Are you serious?"

"I'm serious," he laughs, pulling her close. "What do you say?"

I say, "I've never worked in a store in my life."

"Is that your only concern?" he laughs. "Intensive training," he shrugs, "paid, of course. And I'll be in town for at least a month," he says, "so I can answer any questions you may have, and that's only if Liz here can't."

"I spent so many summers working in stores just like this!" she says to me a little too boastfully.

They're both looking at me, all smiles and bright open eyes.

"I don't know," I say like it pains me more than it does, "I have people and responsibilities back in Los Angeles and there's every chance I'd be making stupid mistakes when it came to cashing up or recommending what kind of lock would be best for certain needs and-"

"Intensive training," Iain grins, "*paid*."

"And I'll have somebody else count the money for you," Liz smiles, "and if I have to, I'll appoint a lock expert, just for you!"

"Come on," Iain says, "you could both start your training next Monday. You could both move into the apartment whenever you decide because I've already paid two months' rent up front as well as even putting a little money to one side for anything you might need; you can pay it back a couple of bucks each week because I would like to know someone is keeping an eye on the place before it opens and I'd like to know the people in charge were people I could trust with my life. You'd be helping me out a lot more than I would you."

"I don't know," I sigh, "can we take a quick look inside the place right now?"

Liz shrieks with delight, comes bounding over to me and wraps her arms around me. She's never held me this tightly. Over her shoulder, I see Iain smiling over at us both.

36

Abigail finally releases the breath she has been holding for far too long and finishes with, "I'll be sorry to see you go."

I reckon there's a little truth in that but a lot of bullshit. She's just sorry I'm going before they've had a chance to catch me doing something wrong. Or at least what *they* view as being wrong, anyway. And she's glad she won't have to be helplessly standing there when Tony at long last returns and kicks my hide out of the door, before her very eyes. Wherever the man is, she's just glad it isn't here- watching her accepting my being so close without question. You just *know* she feels he wouldn't have stood for it... my being here at all, let alone so long.

"I'm sorry," I tell her with a smile, "but I just feel there's nothing more I can do. Even Barbara, that was her name, wasn't it? Even Barbara insisted I stay here to keep an eye on Terry. Barbara *insisted*, Abigail. She wanted me under this roof for one reason and now that reason has gone. There's not a lot I feel needed for, now Terry has gone out to research his masterpiece."

"Yes," Abigail sighs and she brushes a trace of dust from her desk with the side of her hand before looking to me again. "So when will you be going?"

"Let me see," I answer while taking my cigarettes and Zippo from my pocket. I take the cigarette out slow, just in case there's any chance of her missing the action, and tap it twice against the box before lighting up. "I think the removal men are coming tomorrow but let's face it, they have nothing of mine to take. I can throw everything I have in my possession into a paper bag," I smile. "They're coming for Liz's stuff, obviously."

Every time I think I could be enjoying this a little too much, I just remind myself how she asked me to come and see her. I would have happily walked out of the place when the time had come without saying a fucking word but she wanted this. When I first entered the room I was a little nervous. I figured she had a card left to play but it soon became obvious she didn't. Maybe she just wanted to be sure I was going when Liz was, maybe she knew I'd take a little delight in this conversation and then, if all went sour someplace down the line, she could take her own on telling me there was no room at the inn if I ever turned up at the door with my ass in my hands.

"Yes," she says, "Liz will be missed."

"Don't worry," I tell her, "I'll keep an eye on her. Keep her on the right path."

"And I'm sure you will," Abigail says back to me, a smile on her lips resembling a gnarled and twisted branch decaying in winter. "But I wish you both the very best. Now," she asks, "can I count on your continuing support over at the soup kitchen?"

"Not for the foreseeable," I tell her. "We'll both be participating in extensive, work-based training and that won't leave us with much free time, what with also preparing the store and our place to stay."

"Of course," she says, clearly disappointed at the idea of having to find two new suckers. "You should know that any help you could provide us with would be greatly appreciated. This is an old building," she continues, "and the building where we hold our soup kitchens is also in disrepair. Any financial donations or even discount on building supplies or available man hours for repair work on either premises would be greatly appreciated."

Despite it all, I still find myself taken aback at the fact she dragged me here just to try and claim some of my good fortune as her own.

"Well the problem is," I lie, "me and Liz have been talking about the work you have done here and how we could greatly improve it. We were talking about maybe allowing the men to spend the night in the store and maybe even training them up to work for us... Really get them back on their feet instead of giving temporary solutions, you understand? I don't see how we could partner up with you if we all wanted different things," I smile. "And I think people would prefer our way of thinking to your own. I mean, our way wouldn't cost anybody but us a dime."

She makes a clicking sound on swallowing.

"Well there's little more I can do," she says, "than wish you the very best with whatever ventures you should happen to take. Your work here has been greatly appreciated and somewhere in Los Angeles, your church will be sad to see you go. Is there anybody I can contact at all?" She asks, "Is there anybody you would wish for me to speak with? Forgive me but what was the name of your church again?"

"Please," I smile, getting to my feet, "no forgiveness is necessary and I wouldn't want to take up any of the time you have left here."

Take that, bitch.

37

"THERE WAS A queue of people," Iain says excitedly, "going right down the street! I tell you, human resources are going to have boxes of application forms to look through!"

The three of us are sitting in a late-night cafe. Iain had wanted to meet because he said he had good news regarding how people had responded after learning a big store was soon going to open and all manner of vacancies would need to be filled.

Liz and I had downed tools and headed straight out to meet him here. Well, to tell the truth, Liz had downed tools. She's something of an expert with an electric hand drill. She'd already put the new TV on the living room wall and a couple of other things for decoration. I made myself useful by bringing her coffee. And I have to admit, she has the place looking homely. It's just I was wondering what part of it, if any, would ever look like it could be my home. Boxes of Liz's things had arrived a couple of days earlier. A lot of books, hundreds of records, small furniture, clothes; the things a person gathers during their lifetime. All I'd needed to do was go out and buy a new rucksack to carry my few possessions over to the place. And we share a bedroom despite there being two... I just don't know what we'll say if Iain ever goes and asks about our sleeping arrangements.

Liz grins and asks, "Do we get to interview them?"

"Don't you worry about that," Iain assures her, "I'll have my people find the right people for you. You'll meet them all at training over the next week," he says, "you can tell them it's just a refresher course for you both or something."

Liz releases a short whistle. "I don't know," she jokes, "lying to our workforce could be bad for morale..."

"Please," I tell her, "you take hold of any application form that we've been given and I'd bet at least sixty percent of it would be bullshit."

Iain looks at me approvingly, says, "You've got that right," before turning his attention to Liz. "These are very competitive times," he tells her. "People will be falling over themselves for an opportunity like the one we're willing to offer and who cares if a few white lies are told when it is going to end in a thriving economy for towns like this one? Bit by bit, inch by inch, people like us will be making this country proud and strong all over again."

Liz nudges me in the ribs and says, "Forgive my brother- his patriotism shoots through the roof when he's talking business."

"I know," he grins, "I know it might not have all the glamour of the *rock and roll* scene, but honest and clean business just gives me a buzz like nothing else in the world." He lifts his coffee to his mouth but thinks better of it, places it back down on the table. "And isn't that what America is all about? Honesty and hard work being rewarded? The chance of a better life? One man helping his brother and asking no reward?"

"It's not what I'm seeing on the news," I risk saying with a playful smile. "All people seem to care about now is disposable income to spend on short-lived technology, easy access to guns and bombing deserts."

"Well that's not us," Iain says, "because that's not our America. We're here to offer security to you and your family and we don't believe in second chances- we believe in as many chances as it takes."

I don't ask him whether there will be some kind of commission for selling expensive locks over their cheaper counterparts.

38

Iain jumps into a cab to the hotel he's staying at out of town, happy to know he'll be examining application forms and resumes alongside a handful of employees working at double pay for the night. He hands Liz and me money for a cab of our own despite how close we are to our apartment. We get back, talk about how exciting it might be to run our own store and then we head to Liz's bedroom which also doubles as *our* bedroom.

There's a framed poster of a rock show she went to placed directly over the bed- *...And You Will Know us by The Trail of Dead.* I try not to notice it too much because I'm sure the Pennington boy owned a couple of their records and thinking about him only has me thinking about how I was rode out of Whicker with my tail between my legs. When that happens I try to focus all of my attention on him and hope he's treating his mother right but it rarely lasts. My mind wanders to Maria Leeson and I take to wondering how she is. Whether she misses me. Whether she blames her old man for my absence. Whether I punched a hole clean through her family's heart; whether I've been forgotten about like last year's news already.

But under the sheets, Liz isn't as silent in here- not by a long shot. She can get pretty noisy but it's not like she's a wailing banshee.

We fuck and I roll off her after planting a kiss upon the tip of her nose. The air is cold and filled with moisture. A car rolls by outside, lights skimming first along the walls and then the ceiling before vanishing. I light a cigarette without offering Liz one. She hasn't smoked for a few days, says she has a sore throat. She breaks the silence.

"I have something to tell you."

I'm too tired to talk. She knows I'm awake so she continues.

"I'm pregnant," she says.

I'm stiff as a board for a moment. I get up on shaky legs, head over to the window and open it, standing there stark naked. "That could be good news," I tell her.

"It might not be yours."

"Doesn't matter," I tell her.

"I just had to tell you."

"I know," I sigh, "I know. It could work," I tell her. "You're mine and, as far as I'm concerned, the baby is mine."

Liz gets up out of the bed, walks over and stands with her arms around me.

39

Verne is one of the people working at the store I feel closest to. He's got a decent sense of humour and he has seen a lot of films. He's waiting outside as I arrive; his bike leaning against the wall with his high visibility jacket over the handlebars but he's still wearing the helmet. Noticing how he still has at least half of a cigarette to smoke, I slow down a little and delve a hand inside my own pocket to have one alongside him before going in. You just have to hope the conversation isn't awkward at times like this. It doesn't matter how much you like a person you work with, you just feel you *have* to talk about something from time to time when it would be better to simply keep your eyes open.

"Verne," I greet him with a nod, "you been here long?"

"About a minute," he says with a shake of his head.

"Not too bad," I shrug, leaning my back against the wall and lighting my cigarette. It's a cold morning. Mist comes from your mouth whenever you talk. "How's Emma?"

Emma is the name of his girlfriend. She pops into the store from time to time and it's near impossible to take your eyes from her. She's twenty-four but she looks around sixteen. I envy him for the fact he gets to see her naked; gets to sleep with one arm around her so he can feel a little tit during the night.

"She's good. How's Liz?" He asks, "She coming in later today?"

"She isn't feeling too good," I tell him and I leave it at that instead of letting him in on how we haven't been talking for the last week or so. It's gotten so bad that Iain managed to pick up on it over the phone. Can you imagine that? Man's in a different state and even he knows something isn't right. I told him what she can be like and he just laughed it off. "Why do you think some of the people who know her better than anybody else in the world call her Liz or Beth instead of just settling on one?" he asked. "It's a joke someone made when we were still kids; said there was three of us instead of two - one of the girls was evil," he laughed. "Liz and Beth," he finished, "but nobody could decide which was the good one and which was the evil one."

Verne grins and says, "Can't blame her, right? Isn't she due to drop any day now?"

"Any day now," I repeat back at him with a nod.

"You excited?"

"Yeah," I smile.

"You decided on any names yet?"

"Liz wants Tiffany for a girl but I'm not too keen. I kind of regret the decision we made of her naming a girl and me naming a boy now because of it."

"So what're you going to do if it is a girl?"

"I don't know," I sigh. "Deal with it?"

"Yeah," he laughs, "but what can you do? What about for a boy?"

"I don't know," I tell him, "I'm pretty undecided."

40

Doyle's sitting in a chair in the living room with fish dying at his feet. The chair he's sitting in, like him, is soaking wet. His skin's blue but it looks like he's covered it in cheap Halloween makeup. It's a surprise to see him.

"Doyle," I ask him, "what happened?"

"They buried me at sea to save space," he says, water pouring from his mouth. It doesn't sound like he's talking underwater; he doesn't sound any different. "It's a nice place you have here."

"Yeah," I agree, "I like it."

He nods slowly. "I know Cole is still walking around," he says. "You want to explain that?"

"Doyle," I say, "whatever has gone on, don't you think it's about time to forgive and forget?"

"I can't," he says, "and you're the only one who can help me out."

"No," I tell him, "I can't."

"After everything I done for you..."

"I went to jail for you and you're asking me to go back there."

Suddenly, I hear somebody running up the stairs. Sounds like a lot of them, all heading to my front door. Fear takes a hold of my heart. The bolts on the door won't hold them back for anything over a minute. They're here for me. A song I don't recognise starts playing far too loud, coming from all around me.

"You want peace," Doyle says, "you have to do this one last favour for me."

***

I wake up and wonder how I've managed to sleep for so long. My right arm is dead; feels as heavy as a truck. It takes a couple of seconds that feel like hours but my body slowly comes to and joins me here. I sit up and manage not to wake Liz. Every once in a while, her foot twitches. I smile at that. Using the little natural light available I head over to the cabinet on the other side of the room and rummage around the inside of the top drawer.

I know the feel of Doyle's dog collar right away.

It looks blue in the light- somehow cleaner than it should. Just holding it again makes me want to cry.

I head out of the bedroom and into the kitchen, turning on the light. My Zippo is on the table where I left it. I take hold of it and walk on to the kitchen sink.

"I'm sorry, Doyle," I say, flicking the light open, "but I hope this gets you some peace."

I set the collar alight and hold it until the flames are licking at my fingers. The idea of calling the baby Cole if it's a boy comes to mind. One last shot at encouraging Doyle to forgive and forget.

41

"This is what we should have sounded like!" Liz says as if she's experiencing an excruciating pain and is resisting the urge to scream. "Listen to it," she says, "our debut album should have sounded like this but the producer got it all wrong and we were all too scared to set him straight!"

The distress is caused by a record Terry sent to her from wherever. I'd love to put it all down to her hormones being out of sorts with the baby being overdue but I can't. She just gets like this sometimes. And this is the second time I've found her getting all frustrated at listening to Tess Parks' *Blood Hot*. It arrived in the mail just a couple of days ago, another unrequested gift from Terry. Another female performer's name to go alongside Elena Tonra and Sharon Van Etten should I ever make a list titled *Women in Music I Would Rather Be Sharing a Bed With Instead of Liz*. Women of a high enough quality to make up for the disaster I've made of my life up to this point.

"You could always make a record that sounds more like this one," I tell her, hoping the idea will be accepted and give her an excuse to go missing for a while... Say a few months recording it before taking it out on the road.

Even when we're getting on fine, she just makes too much noise. Never wanting to sit in silence and stare at the TV after a long day. It's not even like we're talking business, it's nothing but noise. What she got up to during the day. What she heard on the news report. Who phoned her earlier on.

Her guitar playing I can handle. Sometimes I even enjoy the sound of her strumming away in another room. But the needless talking is getting to be too much for me. I prefer silence.

No wonder the baby doesn't feel the urge to come on out here, it'd only have her talking at it without stopping for air. And the doctor is saying we're on a countdown now... That they'll have to get the baby out one way or another if it doesn't come voluntarily and soon. I told the doctor we're all living longer now, so surely it would make sense if we spent more than nine months in the womb, but he wasn't willing to listen.

"It'll just sound like I'm copying her," Liz says, sounding far too annoyed than she has any right to be. "I don't want her being credited for starting a whole movement."

I'd go outside but it's cold and it's raining so there's nothing I can do but sit down and put up with this. I'd ask Liz if she had made anything for dinner but I know she hasn't because I can't smell anything and asking her would only make her a bigger pain in the ass. She'd start with how difficult it is to be pregnant and how only a sexist asshole would go out to work for some nine hours and expect the dinner to at least be cooking on returning home. Hoping it'll change the subject of conversation, courtesy of a little distraction, I ask, "Have you talked with Iain today?"

"No," she says, turning away from the stereo, "how come?"

Hallelujah, it worked.

"Wondering," I tell her. "I spoke to him this afternoon and he said he was going to call once he got the chance."

"He didn't," she says. "Anything important?"

"No," I tell her, "just asking for a little room to be prepared for some new stock that's coming next month."

42

EVERY WRONG I have ever done, every bad feeling I have ever experienced, they seem to fall right away from me as I stand there holding the sticky newborn. He's so perfect he brings me to tears. I can't help but look to Liz and thank her. She's already smiling at me, her skin red and damp. I sit beside her and start to laugh, making a silent vow to never take her for granted or hurt her for what she has given me.

"It's a boy," she says, placing her head against my shoulder, "now you're going to have to settle on a name."

"How about Cole?"

"Cole Doyle," she smiles. "I like that."

"No," I blush, "don't give him my name. You carried him for nine months, you did all the hard work. Give him your name," I insist.

I'm no big feminist out to do what I think is right; I just think it'd be easier for him to have her name in case they ask for any documents proving my identity. If needs be I'll talk my way out of going onto his birth certificate. I'll say I know in my heart he is mine and that is all that matters.

"Okay," she smiles, and she tenderly strokes at his face.

Looking at him, I can't tell whether he is mine or not. I can't really remember what I used to look like or who I once was. But he does have his mother's eyes.

"Look at him," I say, "he doesn't even have any idea what fear or anger is. Has never had to struggle for anything. Right now," I tell her, "he's the purest thing on the planet."

"We're going to have to call Iain," Liz says, "let him know he's an uncle. He'll probably want to know his weight and exact time of birth," she smiles, "there'll be bets on it over at his office."

"All that can wait," I tell her, "let's just enjoy this for the moment."

43

I HAVE MATT announce over the speakers that the store will be closing in five minutes and all customers should make their way to the cashiers, then I just wander around to try and make myself look busy. Other workers can cash-up today, I'm too tired. I move along various aisles, easing a finger over various price tags to make it look like I'm checking they're all right when I'm really waiting for somebody to let me know the last customer has gone. A figure appears beside me. Black guy, little smaller than me, that's all I take in. I don't look right at him in case he starts asking me for advice or something.

"Excuse me," he says to get my attention. He sounds plenty more African than American.

"Yes?" I ask, straightening my posture while turning to face him with a cheery smile to try and cover how disappointed I'm feeling. How I'm regretting the idea to wait out here instead of hiding out back.

The man is the darkest shade of brown I've ever seen. The whites of his eyes are more of a deep yellow but there are faint traces of red and even greyish-blue here and there. He looks at me with his mouth open- lips almost three sizes too large for his face. "You worked here long?"

I can't figure out why he's looking at me the way he is- what the look could mean- but I go on smiling anyway and point at my badge. "Since the place opened," I tell him.

He looks to the badge, grins and looks me in the eye. "Deputy manager," he says.

"That's me," I tell him.

"Lee," one of the part-timers interrupts, "we have a customer wanting a refund and I can't find anybody else who can do it."

The black guy nods and says, "See you around," before walking away. I watch him moving on until he turns out of sight, trying and failing to understand why he had been looking at me the way he was.

"You okay?" the store employee asks.

"Sure," I tell him, "let's go put that refund through so we can get out of here."

44

He eases up alongside me as I'm heading home with a bag of groceries under each arm, the purr of a well-oiled engine coming from beneath the Charger's gleaming hood. It's the most exciting sound I've heard in a long time. It's a sound that promises adventure and a much needed break from the daily grind.

"How's it hanging?" Peter calls out before I even turn to face him.

"Peter," I laugh, "it's good to see you."

"Tell me about it," he laughs, "I thought you would have moved out to Florida by now to spend your silver days under the sun!"

"Fuck you."

"You kiss your boy with that mouth?" he grins. "Where you heading to? You need a ride?"

"It'd be appreciated," I tell him.

"Hop in," he says, "throw your things in the back."

I squeeze the grocery bags into the little room the back has to offer. It's something I can't help but do now, look at available spaces and try and work out how you're supposed to share it among a family. "What have you been up to?" I ask, climbing into the front seat. It's been months since I last saw him and just being next to him has given me wings. You just know he's going to have stories to tell you. Stories you'd doubt if anybody else claimed them as their own. "And I recognise this," I add, pointing at the CD player. "Daughter, isn't it?"

"Give the man a prize," he laughs, turning back into the road. "How'd you know?"

"Terry," I admit. "He sent a copy of this to Liz a while back."

"How is Liz?"

"She's fine," I answer, deciding not to share the information, we've barely spoken over the last week. "Cole's great."

"Junior," Peter laughs. "He talking?"

"He can say a few words," I say proudly, "but he points a lot and says what he thinks are better names for things around the house."

"It scare you at all," he laughs, "the responsibility?"

"Nah," I tell him. "There's nothing remotely scary in my life right now. It's a set routine."

"Sounds fun. You still living in the apartment facing your store?"

"That's the place."

"Okay," Peter nods. "Listen," he asks, "I have a little something to take care of along the way. You don't mind adding five or ten minutes to the journey, do you?"

"No," I say like it doesn't matter at all, hand reaching for my cigarettes. I'm as good as giving Liz a reason to be pissed right now. And I've no idea how she'll react if I bring Peter inside for a coffee. "Smoke?"

"Please," he says.

I light two cigarettes and hand one over.

"Thanks. You heard about Terry?"

"I don't think so." I ask, "Has something happened?"

"Fuck," Peter laughs, "you honestly haven't heard?"

"No," I laugh, "what is it?"

"Terry's gone nomad," he reveals. "Living on a farm somewhere with some hippy group, married to a girl calling herself Mother Blue."

"I really don't know whether I should believe this or not."

"I swear," Peter says, "it's going on. He's been telling me how wonderful it is- living off the land and being free. I don't know what he's doing for money but he *must* be doing something because he's still using his cellphone, but yeah," he grins, "he even sent me a bracelet he had made himself."

"This is nuts! So what is it," I ask, "some kind of religious cult group?"

"That's the first question I asked," Peter laughs. "He doesn't think it is. From what he's saying, they're just a bunch of likeminded people living under the stars. They even elect the five people who'll be in charge for the good of the group on a bi-monthly basis."

"This is wild. Has Terry thrown his name into the ring?"

"Not that he's admitted. But get this," he says, "they don't touch drink or drugs. Don't even smoke."

"You're shitting me?"

"Nope," Peter says. "He says they're against altering the mind."

<h1 style="text-align: center;">45</h1>

We're slowly headed down a backstreet when two young guys come walking out from behind a large dumpster. They're both tall and skinny, both dressed like they wish they were black gang members. They don't particularly walk into the road than swagger. Peter takes to slowing the car down, raises a hand from the wheel slightly and holds it up with the fingers outstretched. I ask him, "You know these jokers?"

"They're not too bad when you get to know them," he claims.

As we're getting just a couple of feet from the two guys, one of them takes a cellphone from his pocket and backs away to take a call. Peter brings the car to a halt. The one remaining guy heads over to his side of the car as Peter brings his window down.

"Peter, my man," the guy says, reaching in to shake his hand. "What's up?" he asks.

"I'm good," Peter nods before introducing me. "This is Lee," he says. "Lee, this is Bill."

"You the guy that runs the hardware store, right? I got a friend who works there," he says immediately after asking me the question. "I seen you in there a few times."

"Who's your friend?" I ask just to appear polite.

"Dobler," he says. "Unloads the delivery trucks."

"Sure," I smile and nod, "I know who you mean."

"So, you here to pick up or not?" he asks Peter, turning away from me in such an abrupt manner I'm left wondering whether I've passed some kind of test or failed it.

"If you've got what I want," Peter smiles, holding up a carefully folded bundle of notes. Bill looks up and down the street before accepting the cash and immediately stuffing it down the front of his pants. "Always a pleasure," he says, briefly shaking hands with Peter again to hand over something that is quickly slipped under the driver's seat. "Hey," Bill wants to know, "is Terry still

133

saying he's living clean and up on a farm?"

"Yeah," Peter says with a laugh, "he's still living the dream."

"You tell him to call me, would you? Barns are good places to grow some shit and I'd make it worth his while."

The second guy comes walking over from wherever he had disappeared to in plain sight, holding his cellphone at his side. He looks right over me and Peter; taps Bill on the elbow and says, "Fucking Vic was on the phone. Said Jack has been spotted."

"Nigger came up from his hiding place at last? Where's he at?"

I take a gasp for air which thankfully goes unnoticed, wondering if these two bums could be talking about the very same Jack I knew out in Whicker. "Guys," Peter interrupts, "I'll be back soon."

"Sure," Bill says as he reaches in to shake Peter's hand one final time, "you know how you can get a hold of me. Good to meet you," he adds for my benefit.

"And you," I smile back at him. Peter nods to the two men and moves the car onwards as they both back away and get on with their private conversation. I wait until we've turned off the backstreet and are back on a main road before asking Peter if he happens to know this Jack guy they had been talking about. "I don't think so," he shrugs, "I can't remember ever meeting them when they were with somebody called Jack."

"But those two are your friends?"

"I wouldn't say that," he says. "Strictly business."

"Right," I laugh. "So what was it you were buying?"

"Just some shit to keep me alert for the next few days because I have a lot on," he smirks.

"Oh?" I ask him, "Anything serious?"

"Just a couple of papers I have to get done- once I've finally caught up with the reading."

"I ever tell you I never finished high school?"

"It shows. Only kidding," he grins.

Jack from Whicker just leaps right back into my mind without any warning so I can't resist the urge to ask, "But you're sure you don't know who it is they were talking about? You've never seen them hanging out with a guy wearing glasses?"

"Glasses?" he laughs. "I don't think so," he grins. "What makes you ask that?"

"Forget about it," I tell him, "it's nothing. Maybe somebody wearing glasses would be able to convince them they aren't black."

46

I ask Peter, "You ever heard *Wolf Hands* by Zombina and the Skeletones?"

His apartment is small and cramped. He said he only moved here recently and is hoping to have it looking better by the end of the week but space- or lack of it- is going to be an issue. There are lots of plastic crates and cardboard boxes filled with books, CDs and records piled one on top of the other. Getting up from your chair and going to another room is more than a little difficult because of it.

"Sure," Peter says with a nod as he goes on rolling a fresh joint, "fun song."

There's a poster of Lou Reed taking pride of place on the wall, the Transformer cover. Liz has been listening to that album a lot recently and that's just one of the things that's pissing me off. When she's angry or depressed or both, she doesn't stick to music that would best give me a clue about how she's feeling or why. It's like she's just business as usual when she clearly isn't.

"Liz said that's *our* song," I tell him before pausing to wet my throat with a little beer. "You ever seen the video? I looked it up online a while back," I say, "and up until a point it's looking like it could easily be one of the hottest things you could ever see."

Peter smirks, licks the gum of the cigarette paper and says, "Pretty flattering, her saying it's your song and all."

"Yeah," I sigh, "I thought that too."

"You know the Missionaries are leaving town?" he asks me, lighting up.

"No," I smile. "Do you know why?"

"Lack of funds or something. I'm not sure," he says, "it doesn't really concern me."

"I don't think I ever met that Tony."

"You aren't missing anything."

He passes the burning joint over. "Thanks." I tell him. "Before tonight, I can't even remember the last time I touched this stuff."

Peter nods and says, "It's been a long time since everybody got together and now," he sighs, "Terry's out on the frontier or something and you and Liz are part of the perfect family."

"Liz is going to bust my balls if I don't get home soon."

Peter starts laughing uncontrollably, doubling over because of it. I start laughing alongside him.

"It's true," I tell him, "I told her I'd only be gone an hour or two."

He somehow manages to ask through all the laughter, "You got a cell?"

"Turned it off in case she tries calling me," I laugh. "I am in so much trouble..."

Peter falls off the couch for laughing. "I shouldn't be laughing," he says, "because she is going to kick your fucking ass!"

"Tell me something I don't know."

"Jesus," he sighs, wiping a tear from his eye, "when did everybody start growing up? You and Liz," he says, "and even Terry of all people. Man," he laughs, "I've got to hurry up and get my life in order."

"I don't know," I tell him, "I think you've got it better than all of us."

"Nah," he says, "no way. You've gone and done what grown-ups are supposed to do; you have your job and your home and your family..."

"All fell into my lap," I say, "and I don't think I'd have gone out and worked for any of it if I'd had to."

"But you're happy," he asks, "right?"

"Honestly," I tell him, "I don't know. I mean, I wasn't really expecting anything like this. Don't get me wrong, I always just assumed something like this would happen when I was younger, but I can't tell you for sure whether I actually wanted it to."

Peter nods as if in understanding and says, "My cousin got a girl pregnant while they were both young and moved in with her and her parents. I asked him what it was like one day, being a father and all, and you know what he said?"

"What?"

"He told me that all the love and joy you feel on watching your kid grow up, it isn't any different to the way you feel about a family pet."

47

I WAKE UP feeling like shit. My first thoughts are of how Liz is going to have my balls on a stick because I've stayed out but I'm too sore to care. My head feels like a debt collector has been pounding at it with a baseball bat.

Slade are playing on the stereo. I'd heard one of their songs in a dream I can just about remember having. Peter must have put the album on repeat and left it playing all night, seeping into my mind.

My mouth is chalk-dry and tastes like old cigarettes. There's a half-empty glass of something in front of me, a drink I didn't take the time to finish. Getting to my feet has me feeling like I've just stepped off a rollercoaster. I resist the urge to collapse and take clumsy steps to the bathroom. I piss, flush, and splash a little warm water over my face. I look like shit. I don't think I ever looked this kind of bad in all my time with Doyle.

"Peter," I croak, heading towards his bedroom. "Peter," I say a little better, knocking at the door before entering. He's under the covers, packed-in like a butterfly about to emerge from its cocoon. He lifts his head an inch or so from the pillow and rubs his right eye, looking at me. "I'm about to leave."

"Time is it?"

"I don't know," I tell him. "It definitely isn't yesterday."

"Okay," he says, lowering his head back down onto the pillow, "I'll see you soon."

"See you soon," I nod but I don't walk away and leave, I stand there at the doorway and glance around the room. Posters of bands I still haven't heard of despite our friendship and despite my relationship with Liz. One of the larger posters is black and white, a cute girl standing up front with a guy at either side of her. Written in red along the bottom of the poster is what I'm guessing is the name of their band; Churches, but they have a V in place of the U and the E at the end is just three horizontal lines.. "That a band you like?"

"Who?" he asks, sounding more than a little groggy as he struggles to lift his head up from the pillow for a second time. He must have fallen straight back to sleep without either one of us even noticing.

"There," I tell him, pointing a finger to the poster.

"I don't know," he says, "I guess."

"They any good?"

"Only if you're in a good mood," he says with a yawn. "They're not a band to listen to if you're feeling down or weary and I can't see them ever being seen as cool. I only put that up because of the babe."

48

IF IT HAD been down to me, Stan would have lost his fucking job a long time ago. He's a little older than me and he's married with two kids of his own but he's such a fucking weirdo. I told Liz I wanted him gone not long after he'd actually started but she said she couldn't just get rid of him- not with him having a wife and children to support. With Liz not wanting to play ball, I started dropping him on every shitty shift that I could, hoping it would encourage him to go find work elsewhere; but it hasn't happened.

I swear, I'm only on shift with him every now and again but that is more than enough. I just want the asshole gone already. From what I've heard, he's one of those people that always have to match or better a story; you tell him about the time your friend tripped and broke his ankle when he was drunk and he will tell you how it also happened to a friend of his or about the time he tripped when he was drunk and broke both arms.

The man was desperate to get everybody together for a night out and nobody wanted to play ball but eventually he got what he wanted. It was somebody's birthday and something of a staff night out actually took place. I didn't go. I'd said Cole had a fever or some other excuse along those lines and stayed at home, knowing they would all be too loud and too immature for me to handle. I'd spent part of the night laughing with Liz, telling her jokes Verne had made about Stan and looked forward to the start of a new working week because of it.

I'd been sure there'd be fun stories told about Stan... Stories he would be embarrassed about. Stories that would maybe see him taking another job far away from me.

I don't know what the fuck had happened that night but a lot of people suddenly saw him in a much nicer light. Within days people went from thinking he was okay at best to going out for lunch with him. I still don't see it and believe me, I keep a closer eye on him than anybody else. I watch him talking to the girls and you just *know* it's all an act... That he wants to say something real sleazy or take to humping at their leg like a wild dog.

"Hey," he calls out to somebody just out of sight on heading out of the storage room, "that girl you were with the other night is still in there. Toss her out already, she's starting to decompose!"

And suddenly, everything seems right in the world.

Three long days and nights with Liz only acknowledging I'm there when she's telling me to move out of her way (all because, horror of horrors, I had an unplanned night out with a friend!) and now I can return home and tell her I've gone and sent Stan on his merry way. I can return home and have her admit she should have listened to me after all.

"Stan," I say making my way from behind the counter, "a word."

"No problem," he says, all smiles as he turns to face me. "What's up?"

"My office," I tell him, heading for the doors he had just come from, "now."

49

No one hangs around on the street as I lock up for the night. There really is no need for them to anyway but they usually do, making small talk and generally waiting until the shutters are secured before we all go our separate ways. A couple of brief goodbyes and everybody is walking away, scared I'm on a firing rampage or something. It doesn't bother me. I try to get along with everybody but we're not here to make friends.

A car comes over as I'm locking up. At a guess I would say it's one of those electric ones because it's small and the shape isn't too different from your basic cube. It just stands there with the lights on me. I ignore it. The driver steps out. I ignore him, go on securing the locks. Probably somebody convinced they need a padlock a lot more urgently than they really do; someone willing to get into an argument if I don't open up for him to just *pop inside* like it would be that simple.

"Lee."

A voice I recognise. A voice that sounds plenty more African than American.

"Yes?" I ask, keys protruding from a clenched fist. Makeshift *knucks* would be no real use against a man with a gun but I'm not in the mood to care. He just stands there beside his car, engine running and the lights on me. A three dimensional silhouette.

He calls me by a name I haven't heard in a long time. Or at least I think he does, anyway. It's hard to understand, what with the accent. Reaching for my cigarettes I ask him, "Do I know you?"

He comes forward, light finding him long enough to show the grin he's wearing before the light drops back behind him and I'm left standing in his shadow. "We served time together," he says. "You remember?"

"I'm sorry," I tell him, "but I think you have me mistaken."

He puts an open hand against his chest to reintroduce himself. "Justice," he says and right away I remember him.

Justice.

We all called him Justin. His full name was Justice Redemption Something-or-Other. Zimbabwe born, serving time for both drug dealing and sexual contact with a minor (he swore he thought she was eighteen). He was still inside when I was released and I've no idea what he's doing out... what he's doing here instead of being back in Africa.

"Justice," I nod. "What're you doing here?"

He says something I don't quite understand before offering me a ride home. I open my mouth to tell him I only have to cross the street but think better of it.

"Sure," I tell him, "you can drop me off."

"Get in," he says.

50

The streets are all dark, empty and wet. Rain's falling. Not much and not heavy but every drop looks like a machete blade. Justice drives. He rarely asks if we're going the right way and when he does I tell him to take a left or a right if we've been going straight for a while. And his car doesn't seem to have a stereo. He has something I've never seen before; something that looks like a small black circle with wires coming from it that lead to a portable speaker he's taped to the dashboard. That's the source of the music. That's the source of something bland and generic.

"Drink?"

"What was that?" I ask despite hearing him first time around.

"Drink," he says and he lifts a finger from the wheel to point at a bar not too far ahead. He's slowing the car down already so it's not like I have any real say in the decision.

"Sure," I tell him, patting at my hips just to be sure I've got my wallet. "You mind if I have a smoke before we go in?"

"Have it outside," he says on pulling up. "No smoking in the car."

I climb out of the vehicle and light my cigarette. There's a No Smoking sign at the bar entrance. "Shit."

"I'll get the drinks," he says, rushing towards the door. "What do you want?"

It sounds more like an order than a question.

"Just get me a beer," I tell him.

"What brand?"

"Any."

"What?"

"Just anything."

"What?"

"Just get me whatever you're having," I tell him. He looks at me like I'm an idiot, nods with his mouth open and disappears inside. I'd make a run for it if the prick didn't know where I worked.

"How'd you get yourself into this one?" I sigh, looking up to the clouds above and having the cold rain bounce along my face. My cigarette's as good as dead because of the weather so I sigh once again, toss it into the gutter and head on in. The place is pretty empty and you just know the lights are dim to keep you from seeing mould patches climbing the walls. Justice is at the bar, in conversation with a barman who's probably struggling to understand a single word the son of a bitch is saying. I'm glad this wasn't one of my regular haunts. I wouldn't want any of the staff to try and be polite because it would only have the face from my past asking questions about who I would come here with and why I had stopped and the idea of him knowing *anything* else about me isn't a good one.

The barman turns away to fetch the drinks right as I appear at Justice's side.

"Get a booth."

I nod and head for a booth without offering a single word. I watch him pay the barman and collect every cent of his change before making his way over with two bottles of beer and a wild grin. "How long has it been?" he asks.

Not long enough.

"It's been a while," I answer, graciously accepting the beer he eases in my direction. The plan is to drink it as quickly as I can and get out of here.

"You run a store," he says, grinning like it's the craziest thing you could ever imagine.

"Sure do," I nod, swearing to myself I won't tell him about Liz or Cole or any other bit of information he doesn't need to know. "It mightn't be glamorous but it pays the bills."

He nods, still grinning. "I think it is a good thing I saw you."

"Yeah," I lie, "it's good we've got the chance to catch up."

"You can help me out," he says matter-of-factly as he lifts his beer to his swollen lips. A great weight is pressing down on my chest and the son of a bitch hasn't even asked me for a job at the store yet.

"I'll try," I shrug, "but the store is struggling to keep afloat at the minute. If you want a reference or anything like that," I say, "I could make you out to be the model employee."

"No," he says, "it's not a job I need. Money."

The idea of attacking before he has the chance to first crosses my mind. The bottle in my hand could shatter across the side of his skull. I could be bringing his bottle down towards the back of his skull while he's still holding his bleeding face. Jump to my feet, overturn the table to get him pinned against the floor and then it's just a couple of kicks before getting out of there. The only problem is he'd *still* know where to find me.

"It's like I just said," I tell him like it pains me, "the store isn't doing too well at the moment but I could look around," I say, "maybe find someone who could use a hand here and there?"

"No," he smiles, "that's no good. I need the money soon."

"I'm not a bank," I tell him, hoping it'll be enough for him to see how I'm willing to stand up for myself and have him leave me alone because of it.

"You don't understand," he says without losing the smile. "It's not for me."

"Then what is it for?" I ask him like I should give a shit. "You got your girl pregnant or something?"

"No," he says, "it's for Jennings."

"Jennings?"

"Jennings," he says again. "Loyden Jennings."

I sit back in my chair and somehow resist the urge to light another cigarette as I say to him, "Loyden Jennings doesn't exist."

Justice laughs on hearing that. It's high pitched; the notes coming from him in brief, short jabs.

"What's so funny?" I ask. "The man's a myth. It's just a name that gets thrown around inside. No man so well known for whatever could be on the outside of a jail cell. That's not the way the world works."

Nobody inside had met Jennings but they all knew somebody that knew somebody who had. They said he was disfigured because his mom had tried to abort him during the early stages of her pregnancy but he had survived. He went on to choose his own name to distance himself from her- the first person in a long list of many that had tried and failed to kill him.

He shakes his head at my apparent stupidity, downs a little beer and leans in close across the table. I can't help but notice how tightly he's holding that bottle of beer, like maybe he's thinking of bringing it against the side of my skull.

"He's real," he says, "and I owe him."

"He's not real," I insist. "Somebody is just pulling a fast one."

"He's real," he says.

"You met him?" I ask, knowing full well he couldn't have.

"Yes," he nods.

51

Justice goes silent. He wants me to bury him with questions that he has answers he probably decided on in advance but I refuse to play ball. I let him sit there, acting calm and natural, when really my returned silence must be driving him insane. He drums his fingers along the side of his bottle, watches two guys playing pool. I look to the muted TV behind the bar, let the man know I'm not interested in the bait he's dangling.

Tiffany Lily appears on the TV in a bid to sell a new brand of toothpaste. Her eyelids look to be held up with invisible matchsticks, her face puffy in some areas due to whatever she's had injected there. Fuck knows why you'd expect people to notice her teeth when she's had her lips pumped up so badly. I sigh, lifting my beer and say, "I used to know her."

"Right," Justice smirks. "You always said you know everybody."

"No," I tell him calmly, "I didn't."

"Lee with his friends and his big stories," he laughs. "What stories have you been telling lately? What lie did you say when they asked why you had been in prison? What would they say if I told them why you were really there?"

I yawn without knowing I'd needed to, drink a little beer and lean a little closer. "You trying to threaten me?"

"No," he says, eyes fixed on me. "I'm just letting you know how this all ends is in your hands. You give me a little money to get him off my back for a while and I'm gone. You don't and I'm in the hospital recovering for weeks, maybe even months. I could talk to a lot of people during that time... Cops, local press... "

"Because you owe Jennings," I grin, "of course." I drink a little beer and get to my feet. "I'm heading outside for a smoke," I tell him. "I'll have another beer."

"It's your round."

"Come on," I smile, "I'm just the deputy manager of a hardware store- you're the one with ties to the big gangster."

I smile, heading for the door but it doesn't last long. It isn't the sight of the heavy rain that dampens my mood but thoughts of Justice and his far from discreet threats. Turning into the side alley I force myself into the fire exit to find a little shelter from the rain and light a cigarette. The wind howls, changes direction and flicks raindrops into my eyes. I press myself back into the farthest corner to try and get warm. My cellphone vibrates; a message from Liz. She wants to know where I am but I don't reply. I just think about the trouble Justice could cause and try to picture my way out of it. Fuck knows what had him saying I used to come out with all kinds of bullshit. If I had a half decent imagination, I'd have already thought of a way to get rid of him instead of just shivering out in the cold.

"Asshole," I grumble.

A broken figure shuffles into sight; a beaten man walking at a snail's pace. The hood he's wearing is probably up out of habit alone; there's no way the charity store clothes he's wearing are keeping him anything near dry. He stops to the side of me, takes to unfastening his belt with slow fingers and I just stand there watching him, wondering how long it's going to take him to notice me. He takes his pecker out and turns with plans of pissing in the fire exit but jumps back on seeing me, putting his junk back as quickly as he can manage without falling backwards. Man must think I'm security or something.

It's fucking Owen. Or it isn't Owen. I'm not too sure because of the lighting. Or lack of it.

"I know you," he says.

"That's right," I nod as smoke drifts from my parted lips, "through Doyle."

"Yeah," he says, holding a finger in my direction, "Doyle. You know Terry."

"That's right."

"Where's he gone to? I haven't seen him around."

"Yeah," I say, "he's gone."

"Gone where?"

"England," I tell him. "He's got a job as a fashion model or something. Won't be coming back."

"Terry?"

"Yep."

"Oh," he says, lowering his gaze as he looks away in thought. "You got a spare smoke?" he asks, looking back at me.

"Last one," I lie.

"I pay you for it?"

"You want to earn a full pack," I ask him, "make a little money to go with it?"

"What'd you want me to do?"

"There's a cheap-ass car parked out front," I tell him. "You cut the brakes and I'll make it worth your while."

"You serious?"

"Once in a lifetime offer."

"I can't do that!"

"Well how about this," I say, "you hang around and wait for me to come out. You take care of the guy I'm with. Rough him up a little. The bigger the beating, the bigger the payment. All you have to do is bring him down a couple of notches."

"I can't do that!"

"Fuck you can't. I've heard of the videos - people like you fighting for a cheap bottle of wine or something along those lines. I'm offering you a lot more than that."

"You're crazy," he says, shaking his head and backing away.

"Well ask any of your friends if they'd be interested," I tell him as he starts walking away. "Bitch," I mutter as he keeps on going without once looking back. I look down to the cigarette I've wasted; the cigarette looking like a burning filter and nothing more. "Son of a bitch," I sigh, flicking it at a puddle as quickly as I can. I don't light another; I just wrap my arms around myself and rush back to the entrance.

52

JUSTICE SEES ME returning, says something down his cellphone and quickly returns it to his pocket. There's a fresh bottle of beer waiting for me, like a couple of beers is all he needs to get me doing whatever he needs doing.

I think of Liz and how she can be. How I would never really be able to think of her as highly as I probably should unless I were to walk out and never see her again because I'd rather long for her than put any real effort into our shared life. I think of Cole, try to name one worthwhile thing I can ever really offer him. Look at how young he is and I've already got somebody threatening to pull my life apart. I could try and try but all that would happen is I'd drag the kid down and ruin his life or I could just leave him with some minor wounds that never fully heal but come close enough. Loved ones are better without men like me, even if they can't always see it. Men like me can never stay around. We always want what we've lost and if we get it back it won't take us too long to start thinking about how we were better off without it after all, despite how hard we try and convince ourselves different.

"Let's say I'm listening," I tell him, "let's say I'm believing your claims," I add despite the fact I don't, "what is it you'd be expecting from me, exactly?"

"Money," he grins, "just about as much as you can get me from the cash registers and the safe you'll have in the store. You give me everything that you can and you never need to see me again. "

"How about we split it sixty-forty in your favour even though it'll be me taking the big risk here? "

His eyes light up in the darkness. "That could work. "

53

I HAVE JUSTICE drop me off near Peter's apartment. The plan's simple. A quick stick-up job the following night. We meet the following morning, split the money and head our separate ways. The only thing I have to keep him from running out early is the threat I'll make an anonymous call to the cops and tell them who was behind the robbery.Liz was always a beautiful lie. I can never have a life with anything or anybody else. I can never settle down because I'll only drive myself insane if I try sticking with someone. The nearest thing to happiness will mean staying on my own despite whatever else I try to convince myself. The girl, the kid and the steady pay from a job that depresses is just another cell to me. I deserve more, even if more is less.

"Lee," Peter says greeting me, eyes red from whatever he's been smoking or swallowing or both, "come on in." Whatever he's playing on the stereo, I can't name it.

"This a bad time?" I ask him. The windows are open but you can't miss the smell of pot.

"No," he says, "no. Take a seat and I'll get us a drink."

I sit down and he heads out of the room. Noticing a magazine to one side of the couch I pick it up and turn it around to look at the cover. The title makes me smile; Bra-Busting Brit Babes. The girl on the front is more than a little good looking. More than well endowed.

Nude British girls, I'm not complaining but why must you keep appearing in my life?

In need of a little visual appreciation I start looking through it, making the mistake of reading the little extra information they give on the girls inside- their ages. They all seem to be in their early twenties. You know you're getting on in life when you're older than the topless models and the porn stars.

Peter comes back into the room without me even noticing until he opens his mouth to say, "Check out the centre pages and tell me if you can decide who has the best rack; Louise Porter or Brookie Little."

"You remember Quantum Leap?" I ask without looking away from the magazine.

"Yeah," he nods, "of course."

"You ever think about what it would be like if you could leap into your younger self? Live major parts out differently and hope for the best?"

Peter lights a cigarette for himself and tosses one over in my direction. "That'd be some cool shit."

"You think? I kind of worry that-"

"Baby," she says, walking into the room without any idea that I was in there. Fresh out of the bath and wearing a robe as she rubs at her right nostril. She jumps a little in surprise before laughing. "I didn't know you had a friend here," she says.

Whoever she is, she's beautiful. Almost Tori Trumanbeautiful.

"I'm sorry," I tell them both, getting to my feet, "I didn't know you had plans."

"It's cool," Peter says with a wave of his hand, "don't worry about it. We're about to go for a few drinks if you want to come along?"

"Some other time," I say, heading to the door, "but I'll definitely see you soon."

54

"Lee," Verne asks, finding me at his front door, "what're you doing here?"

He's probably trying to remember when and why he gave me his address. He didn't. I went back to the store and looked over the personal information we keep back in the office. I have to wonder how he can afford a nice little place like this. He's probably wondering why I'd come by so late and in this wet weather.

"I was passing by," I tell him, "running a couple of errands and-"

"Verne," I hear his girlfriend call out, "who was at the door?"

He says, "Hold on a sec," before turning around to yell, "it's Lee- from the store. Just hold on one minute."

He steps outside, into the rain, closing the door behind him as if we're going to discuss secret things. He asks me, "Is anything wrong?"

Everybody seems willing to share their life with someone else. Everybody but me.

"No," I tell him, "everything's fine. It's like I said; I just had a couple of things to take care of and was passing through the area. You have any plans for the night?"

Maybe I just think I can't spend my life with somebody else because it can be hard work. Personally, even the noise is too much. Sometimes- most of the time- I'd love to just sit there in silence with something bad on the TV but Liz insists on talking. Long stories you think will never end. They're never as funny as she seems to believe they are.

"Plans? Not really," he says, "we just ate and were about to put a movie on. Take it easy... You know how it is."

"Yeah," I nod, "yeah. What movie are you planning on watching?"

"I don't know," he grins, "some romantic comedy."

"That's what they're like."

"Yeah," he laughs, "that's what they're like."

We stand there for a moment, just smiling and nodding back to one another. I decide to light a cigarette and say, "You think you can get away with skipping the movie? Come grab a few beers?"

"I don't know," he says like it pains him. "We've barely seen each other this week and-"

"Some other time," I shrug, backing away from his home. From his little piece of comfort.

"Definitely," he says. "We'll sort something out at work- get a good group of us together."

"Sure," I tell him, "boost morale."

"I'll see you soon."

"Sure. Have a good night."

"And you."

Why is it I can only seem to handle being on my own? Is it just a lazy choice? If I made the decision to *really* knuckle down, to just focus on the good and let the brief annoyances and other issues rush by at record speed, could I change my life for the better? Could I become a better person?

55

I'M HEADING UP the stairs, up to our apartment, and I can't even remember coming in through the front door. These stairs have always felt too steep. A long and thin crack running along one of the walls has always had me fearing it might collapse on me one day, burying me alive.

Liz is home. I can hear a Pete Yorn record playing in the living room. His third, maybe fourth album. I close the door behind me louder than I have to, just to announce my presence. She doesn't come running out at me to bitch about how she hasn't been able to get a hold of me. I sigh, light a cigarette and head to Cole's bedroom- stubbing the cigarette out against the door before going in. Boy's fast asleep. Angelic looking. He has a lot of his mother's features. I still don't know for sure whether the others are even mine. *"Someday,"* I whisper, *"you'll be the man I could never be,"* and I smile without knowing for sure why and leave the room, softly closing the door behind me. I head into the living room just as quietly. Liz is sitting on the couch, record playing with the TV muted so she can watch the moving images. Neither one of us says a single word. I fall back into the recliner that somehow became my own and relight my cigarette.

"Stan came by a little earlier," she says without first taking her eyes from the TV. Who the fuck is Stan?

"That's nice," I sigh. More than anything, I just want to sleep. Sleep always gets your thoughts clearer and in a reasonable order.

"I've been trying to get hold of you ever since," she says. Her voice is calm, quiet.

"Something important?"

She finally turns her head to look at me. Careful, rehearsed movements like we're on a soap opera. "He told me you fired him."

Ah, now I know who it is we're talking about.

"Yeah," I sigh, leaning back into the comfort of my chair, "that's what I did," I confirm, rubbing at my closed eyelids. "Stan's gone," I tell her, "Stan is no more."

"You want to tell me *why* you terminated his employment."

Terminated his employment. It's enough to make you laugh, this workplace talk.

"Inappropriate behaviour while on the shop floor."

"So nobody is allowed to fool around at the store these days?"

"Not if there's a chance it will offend the public, no."

"He said there was nobody around and it sounds like all he did was make a funny remark to one of his co-workers."

"He would say that."

"What's *that* supposed to mean."

"Jesus," I sigh, "why are you making such a big deal out of this?"

"Big deal?" she snaps. "You're the one making *big deals* out of things when you terminate a man's employment without running it by me first."

"Fuck," I sigh once again, rubbing at my temple. "You've really no clue or even respect for all the things I've done for you."

"What you've done for me? What about everything I've done for you?" she asks. "All of this," she says, "all of this is because of me!"

"And don't I know it. So what's the big fuss about Stan? You fucking him or something?"

"I can't believe-"

"One of you has to be," I shout over her, "for this to be such a big fucking issue. So which one of you is it? Which one of you is it I'm even talking to right now?"

She gets to her feet, walks over and slaps me across the cheek. "You're an asshole, " she says, "and me and your son will be at Joanne's until you're ready to apologise.

Joanne? Some parent from Cole's pre-school activity club, I guess. I don't care. I leave her to pack up her bag and head out with the boy even though it's cold and it's dark and it really should be me leaving. It'll be better not having her around right now anyway.

56

THE LAST CUSTOMERS of the day make their way out of the store and the doors are quickly locked behind them. Everybody is under the impression I've been quiet because of an argument with Liz. Not one of them suspects my rucksack is already packed with a few pieces of clothing, waiting for me beside the bed in an apartment right across the street.

I won't have to ignore that itch for much longer. Soon this place and all the responsibilities that come with it will be nothing more than a memory.

"Okay, " I say on bringing my hands together, "let's get those cash registers dealt with and the stock ready for a new day. "

I make my way to the back of the store, leaving the grunts to deal with the grunt work. Verne is sitting at one of the computers, going through the numbers on the system. He'll probably be store manager come the end of the week. It's something meaningless but he'll be proud and happy with the extra money to bring home. I stop and ask him, "How are we looking? "

"We have a couple of new top-sellers, " he replies once he's pulled the pen from his mouth, "but we're down on sales compared to last week. "

"We have a couple of days left to get the numbers up," I shrug, heading over to the emergency fire exit and deactivating the alarm. "You coming out for a smoke? "

"I'll be with you in a minute, " he says without turning away from the computer screen.

I step outside into the cold night air and light a cigarette. Justice peers out from behind a dumpster in the alleyway, comes rushing over as silent as he can manage once he's sure it's me. His disguise is pretty worthless- sunglasses with a baseball cap but nothing else to hide his features. He isn't even smart enough to wear gloves. I notice that despite the fact he's carrying a handgun- a .38.

It isn't a particularly accurate gun and it isn't one you'd take on a hunting trip but it's popular all the same because it does the job. Even Nick kept one beneath the loose floorboard beside his bed.

"Who's there?" I ask solely for Verne to hear.

Justice swings the gun to the side of my face- a little too hard for my own liking but at least it'll look more believable. My legs buckle. I drop down with my head spinning like crazy. "Get the fuck up," he hisses into my ear, "work with me on this!"

He marches me into the store with his arm around my neck and the .38 pressed to my cheek. Verne turns, takes a gasp and gets to his feet with his hands in the air. Justice points the gun at him and asks, "There an alarm back here?"

He knows there isn't. I told him how the only alarms are situated at the front of the store.

"No," Verne says with a shake of his head.

"You'd best not be shitting me or I'll blow this cracker's fucking brains out! Head out front," he says, "slow and quiet!"

Verne leads the way, slow and quiet like he was asked, hands still high in the air. It only takes a couple of seconds before the first member of staff sees what's happening and screams. The others freeze, turn to see what's going on and stand there with their mouths hanging open.

"Don't anybody do anything stupid now or I'll kill this prick and then I'll shoot this other asshole," Justice calls out, "Just bag up the money from the cash registers and bring it on over and there'll be no trouble. If anybody gets hurt here it's because someone has tried being smart and you can never win an argument with a gun."

Nobody moves. I swallow and say, "Do it." They take to emptying the cash registers on my command, not his.

"You," he says to Verne, "that safe in the back have a time delay or shit like that?"

It doesn't. Iain had been sure that such precautions were unnecessary in a town like this and Justice knows it doesn't because I've told him so now I'm left praying Verne doesn't try to be smart here and lie. "No," he says and relief washes over me.

"Then go empty it and wait for us all to join you back there once you have it bagged, asshole."

Verne looks to me like he's scared this is the last time he'll ever see me and then he goes rushing back, out of sight. I watch as my model employees, filled with fear, load paper bags with the day's takings at record speed.

57

Liz sounds like she's close to tears when she calls.

"Thank God you're okay!" she says as soon as I answer. "Iain called- told me there was an armed robbery at the store?"

It only makes sense Iain would call her. Verne had called the cops once Justice had made his exit and more than four patrol cars had arrived within a matter of minutes. Then the specialists came to dust for prints. The cops took each of our statements and then went over them with us, just to be sure they had everything. I played the man in shock and let Verne keep control of the situation. It was because of him the cops said they would be getting in touch with Iain. Iain had called to check I was okay not long after I'd made it back home and said he would be down the following afternoon.

"I'm fine," I tell her, wandering around the apartment just to be sure I have everything ready for the morning. I pick my cellphone up from the coffee table and drop it into the wastepaper basket alongside my wallet. "Nobody was hurt."

She says, "Iain said you might have a concussion?"

"I'm fine, I really am," I tell her, "the cops said I might want to be looked over because the son of a bitch hit me but it's no big deal."

"I can't believe this has happened." She asks me, "Do they have any idea who might have done it?"

"I don't know," I sigh, "I mentioned the bums sleeping out on the A71 or whatever and they said they'd look into it but if you ask me," I say, lighting a cigarette, "the robber will be long gone."

"Well I'm coming home," she says, "tonight."

"Don't," I tell her. "It'll mean waking up Cole and bringing him back here when you're upset and there'll be an atmosphere. That won't be good for the boy."

"But you've been robbed!"

"And I'm fine," I tell her. "Look- just let him have a quiet night and try and get some rest. Iain will be here tomorrow afternoon, so just get here for when he arrives, Let Cole think it's some kind of surprise party or something."

"I don't know…"

"Liz, I'm fine," I insist. "Things could have been a lot worse. Just wait until tomorrow."

"You really think…"

"Yes. The worst part is already over. Now just try and get some sleep," I say, "and I'll try and do the same once I've had a long bath."

"If you think that's best…"

"It is," I tell her. "Just try and stay calm…. There's really nothing to be upset about."

"Okay," she says, "I love you."

"And you."

58

THE JOKE OF a car that Justice insists on driving is parked right outside his motel room, the sunglasses and baseball cap he had worn during the robbery left on the dashboard for all and any to see. "Fucking idiot," I mutter and I knock at the door of his room.

He doesn't answer. I'm left wondering if the cops have pulled him in already or whether he's skipped town with my share of the money.

I knock a little louder, light a cigarette and get to pounding away against the door. At long last he opens up and I rush inside, pushing the door shut behind me. There's the stench of piss and sweat in the air of the cramped room; a drawer from the dressing table is on the bed to be used as an ashtray. There's a spoon in there... A light and a small ball of aluminium foil. I turn to Justice and look at him. He's wearing a pair of stained underwear and torn socks and that's all.

"Look at you," he grins on spotting the bag over my shoulder. "You really moving on?"

"That's right," I nod. "Where's my money?"

"I'll go get it for you. You got a spare smoke?"

"Last one," I tell him.

"Right," he nods, smiling but making it easy for me to know he sees a lie. "Let me go get it for you," he says and he walks right over the bed and stumbles into the bathroom. "Where you planning on heading?" he calls out.

"Here and there," I sigh, "I don't know yet."

"World's your oyster," he smirks, returning with a crumpled paper bag in his hands. I'm just glad to see he isn't carrying the gun. But then again he probably left it on the passenger seat.

"Your cut," he says, handing me the bag, "like we agreed."

"Thanks."

I relieve him of the bag, open it up and take a look inside, pushing crumpled bills around like it'll help me see how much exactly is there. At a guess I'd say somewhere between two and five hundred. There would have been more than five hundred in the safe alone and we definitely took a lot more than two hundred dollars yesterday.

"I took the coins," he says, "thought you'd want to carry light."

"No sweat," I tell him and we both stand there until I ask, "so what're you going to do now?"

"This and that," he says with a shrug, lowering himself down on the bed. "Disappear for a while. I always thought the trick is to keep moving."

"You don't have to convince me of that," I smile. "See you on the other side, Justice."

"May the Lord carry you," he says and he offers me his hand. Despite my better judgement, I accept it. His palm is clammy and warm. It reminds me of how Doyle would wipe his hand against his trousers whenever it had touched Chambers'.

"Keep safe," I tell him and then I'm gone, closing the motel door behind me and walking on- looking back just to be sure nobody saw me here. I wait until the second payphone before calling 911 and asking for the law.

"Yes," I tell them, "I'm just calling because there's a man staying in the motel on Fifth."

"And what's your concern, sir?"

"Well," I say, lighting a cigarette, "he nearly crashed right into me a little earlier. I followed him because I thought he might be under the influence and he climbed out of the car in nothing but his underwear, sunglasses and a baseball cap. He was carrying a gun and when he saw me looking at him, he pointed it right at me. I just had to drive away as fast as I could."

"And is he still at the motel?"

"I don't know," I tell them, "but I think somebody should get there before he starts shooting," and I put the receiver down and get back to walking.

59

THE COACH HEADING for *Christ-knows-Where* is rolling out of Tryfords when I finally remember to check my rucksack. It's in there, like I knew it would be because I knew I would need it now more than ever. The clerical collar. Just looking at it after so long convinces me everything is going to go just fine. The guy sitting in front of me- the guy who opted to sit right in front of me even though every seat but my own had been available- turns around and shoots me a mean look.

"Are you laughing at me?" he snarls.

"What? No," I tell him.

"You'd best not be," he says, turning back around. You'd think that would be it but it isn't. "I don't care if I am sixty-five," he continues, "I'd fucking rip you down to size. Cheeky motherfucker, I'll fucking shoot you. Cheeky fucking cunt. Who the fuck does he think he is?"

I shake my head in astonishment, lean back in my seat and press my head against the cold window beside me, closing my eyes. The last thing I do before willing sleep to come is slip a hand inside of my pocket to make sure the money won't fall out along the way.

60

I DON'T CATCH the name of the place the coach is stopping in. I just wake up and realise it's mid-morning and my face is more than a little warm from being in the sunlight for so long. The crazy son of a bitch is still sitting right in front of me, probably sleeping himself, and the money is still in my pocket. The driver stops at the designated stopping point and says, "Well, here we are," on looking back through the rear view mirror. I stretch, get to my feet and make my way down the aisle- thanking him before stepping off. We're in a quiet town centre someplace and there's a chill to the air. An old lady sitting on a bench is throwing breadcrumbs down for the gathering army of pigeons at her feet. There are so many around her that they're falling over one another. I light a cigarette, take a quick look around me and start moving towards a diner out in the distance for a bit of breakfast.

61

THERE'S A MAN with a microphone and a portable amplifier but he isn't singing for money. I watch him make claims about how Jesus can grant eternal life and that the Bible tells us we're damned if we don't listen to what it says. He has a couple of people with him, some carrying signs and all trying to hand out pamphlets to people just trying to pass them by. There doesn't seem to be any hope in what the man is selling, just a lot of threats. I stand back and light a cigarette to see if there's anything I can learn from his sales pitch anyway.

"That young child," he screams as a young mother passes him by with her young infant in a buggy, "will burn in Hell if he is not brought to Jesus and his love!"

The mother gives a look of horror and quickens her pace. If anybody else heard what he said, they don't seem to show it. I go on watching and notice a small, chubby guy in a duffle coat heading over with his eyes locked on me and something of a smirk on his face. I figure he has to be one of Captain Crazy's apostles because he looks like a potential psychopath.

"He's got it all wrong you know," he says, standing at my side, his eyes now focusing on the preacher.

"I'd sure like to think so."

The man laughs like I've said something real funny and nods, just keeping his eyes on the hateful man of God. "He's got it all wrong," he says again. "Time's a circle," he adds second time around.

"What makes you say that?"

"Because it is," he says, turning to face me. "It's like the changing of the seasons. We're born, we live and we die. Over and over and over. We'll always do what we're doing right now, nothing major ever changing... Just the same mistakes over and over again."

"Well," I sigh, "that's pretty depressing."

"Isn't it?" he snorts. "And even when we're alive," he says, "it's practically the same thing over and over again when you stop and think about it. You meet someone and you fall in love and then you breakup and then you meet someone and you fall in love and then you breakup. Do you see what I'm talking about?"

"A little."

The man nods, looks to the preacher and then back at me. "You have a smoke?"

"Sure," I nod and I hand him a smoke.

"Light?"

I let him get his cigarette going on the flame of my Zippo and then I'm moving all over again.

62

The bus reaches the end of its route and starts all over again from the beginning.

Public buses- you have to admire them.

Buy a ticket and sit down low at the back to keep out of the driver's sight. As long as people are constantly getting on and off, the driver will forget all about you and you can spend all day there. Some of them run for a solid seventeen or so hours a day. Could be the best way to learn your way around a new town or get a little shut eye. When we're nearing a building we've gone by a couple of times already, I get off to investigate. Looks like it would have been a public building before it was abandoned. There isn't a saint's name anywhere near it.

Iron sheets have been screwed to the door. Someone has tried to remove a bright sticker reading ALL VALUABLES HAVE BEEN REMOVED FROM PREMISES.

The door is secure but the window beside it doesn't even have any glass left in it, it's crazy. I take a quick look around for witnesses before climbing in. Green and black tiles on the floor, gang-tags and slogans covering once white walls. Place smells old and dusty but dry. There's a radiator running the length of the room but it's stone cold. "Could be worse," I shrug, walking on.

The green and black tiles run through every room apart from the bathrooms where they are replaced by red tiles. A mummified shit has been left in one of the urinals. I press down on the cold water tap and it sputters before a steady flow of discoloured water begins to pour. It's as good a place as any to get your shit together.

I turn to make my way back out. Get a little lunch and waste the day before coming back here for the night.

<h1 style="text-align:center">63</h1>

"Treating the girlfriend?" the cashier asks, bagging up the dozen red candles and two bottles of wine I'd handed over.

"You bet," I smile, handing him the money for my items.

"And here's your change," he grins, "don't do anything I wouldn't do," he adds with a wink.

I make my way back to the forgotten public building and check there's nobody watching before climbing in through the broken window. My footsteps echo a little louder than before so I freeze, listen out for the sound of somebody coming to investigate before moving forward again. Cool air is circulating. It might have been an idea to look behind a couple of stores for some discarded boxes but it's too late for that now, I don't want to go on another little adventure now that I'm here.

The rooms get darker as I venture farther in. It's more than a little unsettling, being here alone, so I light a cigarette to steady my nerves and settle on a room that could have been a private office for somebody important long ago. I flick the light switch a couple of times before realising there's no light bulb. I stick my head back out onto the corridor and see they've all been taken.

"Cheap bastards," I sigh, closing the door over to try and keep a little warmth in. There's a pane of frosted glass in the centre of the door; something not to look at as it gets darker because I'll only end up seeing darkened faces staring back at me. I sigh again, get back against the farthest wall and open the first bottle of wine. The candles can wait a while longer- now I just have to get as comfortable as I possibly can.

"This one's for you," I say, taking my first mouthful, not entirely sure who it is I'm actually toasting. It isn't much of a compliment anyway, the wine tastes like piss.

The wind takes to howling outside. It's soon accompanied by wild rain or even hail, which seems a little out of season. Tonight's going to be a rough night and I quickly down a little more wine because of it. If I had an iPod or whatever, even something like Justice had, this wouldn't seem so bad. The music would be a welcome distraction. Songs of loss to convince me I should have maybe tried staying with Liz even though it could never have worked out between us. It could never have worked because I'm not the kind of person to ever want them to. I'm just a man running from one trouble to the next, never having the courage to stand them down.

64

I WAKE UP and forget whatever it was I had been dreaming about and wonder if it was the dream that has me feeling so spooked or something else. It's too dark to see anything. I'd blown the candles out for fear of setting myself on fire and now I'm regretting it more than anything else. Looking to the frosted pane of glass I see a moving dim light which suddenly becomes a lot brighter as it shines in on me. My heart jumps as I try to scramble to my feet. The door opens and the beam of a torch finds my eyes and as good as blinds me.

"What the fuck," somebody mutters from behind the light. "The fuck are you doing here?" he says loud enough for me to hear. "You can't be in here."

"Fuck off," I growl, feeling both a little hungover and a little drunk, "this is my room."

"This is your last chance," he says, coming closer, that light he's blinding me with becoming all the more painful, "get the fuck out of here before I have to get rough with you."

He doesn't realise I couldn't get out of here even if I wanted to- that fucking light is stopping me from seeing the door or how to get around him without risking a knife to the side.

"This is my room," I say, moving forward, the plan being to shove him to the floor and make as quick a getaway as I can. "This is my room."

The light rushes across the ceiling as he uses the torch as a club, hitting me across the head with it. I stumble, almost drop to my knees, and take a hold of his wrist to stop him doing that a second time. Then I rush him towards the nearest wall. I hear the thud as he hits it. I reach for his throat and he drives a fist into my nose. I almost thank the Lord there and then that it hasn't broken for a fucking change. He releases the torch. It rolls out of the room. I manage to land a punch to his balls but it doesn't do much; we both have a lot of adrenaline surging through us. Our tussle becomes nothing more than grappling with the occasional punch thrown here and there, each of us breathing heavily through gritted teeth.

"Wrong move, preacher!" a second voice says. Instantly recognisable but I don't know how. I don't even know for sure where this new arrival is until strong hands take a hold of my arms and pull me away from the person I'd been struggling with. Before I'm hurled out of the room like a sack of garbage, the original attacker throws a punch to the side of my head for good measure.

I hit the wall and fall to my front. This latecomer is strong- you can *feel* his presence as he gets closer and I'm left regretting the fact I didn't buy a knife or something I could use here back when I had the chance.

I'm struggling to pull myself back up when a foot crashes down on my lower back. The air is knocked clean out of me, my spine hurts like hell. Before I can recover, a foot bites into my sides and then blows come raining down on my body. This is a fight I have no chance of winning. Pretending to be somewhere between unconscious and conscious, I take to crawling away- hoping the strong guy won't see any fun in beating on me and will let me crawl out of here with my tail between my legs. It kind of works. He only walks alongside me, kicking at my ribs, with a slight interest. I keep on crawling as best I can. The rucksack containing most of my possessions is lost to me now, I have to admit it.

"Stupid asshole," the larger of the two says on turning away from me- finally losing interest and returning to his friend, "I can't believe he tried that shit."

I keep crawling until I'm sure I'm out of sight then I force myself up and run as best as I can for the exit, tumbling out of the broken window and into the howling winds and rain. They sting my face and I just stay there for a while, motionless and broken. I feel at my throat to loosen the shirt around my neck and realise I'm wearing the clerical collar... must have put it on while I'd been drinking and clean forgot about it.

"Doyle," I groan, "why the fuck couldn't you teach me how to be more like you?"

The wind howls in response. Maybe it's even laughing at how I've always been afraid of one thing or another and will never have it in me to change that.

65

The waitress turns and sees me for the first time. Her mouth falls open a little. She isn't sure whether she should ask me what she *really* wants to ask me. She doesn't want to offend or get involved.

I slept under a bridge to try and keep out of the rain- a broken heap at the roadside. A part of me had wanted to head back to the building I'd been forced from. I'd wanted to go back for the rucksack I'd left behind and to go for round two with the invisible man who'd handed my ass to me without even breaking a sweat.

That's why I'd walked so far away from the place. I didn't want to go back and have the shit kicked out of me a second time. Second time, they mightn't have even let me walk out of there.

I'd been having some crazy dream about Clint Eastwood giving a lecture on how to find closure and posing for pictures alongside me with the theatrical poster for High Plains Drifter at our backs before waking up convinced somebody had tossed a bucket of water over me. They hadn't. A car had gone by, hit a puddle and the water had splashed me. Maybe the driver had done it intentionally, maybe he hadn't even seen me. Who knows?

"What can I get you?" the waitress settles on asking.

"Black coffee," I tell her, "bacon and eggs."

"Coming right up," she says, "go find yourself a seat."

The diner is empty so it's easy to spot the table holding a forgotten newspaper. I make my way over to it and start leafing through the pages with no real interest for what I find. There's an interview with Katy Perry, like whatever she has to say could ever be important. Even the picture alongside the text, clearly taken while she was performing onstage, is enough to have me shake my head. She has her hair tied back too tight to be pretty, is dressed in a sparkling cat-suit and pulling a moronic expression. I would've married her once but now I'd struggle to even jerk off over her. I can't help but picture how everything good of hers must be starting to loosen and drop now; imagine how her sense of humour would always be fart gags. Can't help but think of that poor-selling, God-bothering record of hers from the start of her career that Liz told me about...

I turn the page if only to try and get Liz from my thoughts. I light a cigarette and take my first drag.

"I'm sorry," the waitress calls, "but you can't smoke in here."

"No problem," I sigh, killing my cigarette with the underside of the table before returning it to my packet for later. The waitress comes over with my drink and morning meal, walking away before I have the chance to ask her why the food looks a little strange. I look to the signs above the counter and regret not looking sooner. It's all smiley faces and *Veg. Bacon and Sausage!* and *Free-range Eggs!* and *Fresh Soy Milk!*

Only I'd have the misfortune of finding somewhere like this so far from Hollywood. I start eating anyway because I'm hungry and cold. I start eating even though I know the taste of artificial bacon will stay with me for the entire day.

"If you don't mind my saying," the waitress says as she starts cleaning the tables, "you look like you've had a rough night."

"I've had worse," I tell her.

"But it's all sorted now," she asks, "right?"

"Almost," I tell her, "I just have one last thing to do," I reveal to her as the thought reveals itself to me for the first time. No, not for the first time. It's almost been with me since the very start- it's just I've been too scared to admit it until now.

"Oh," she asks, "and what's that?"

66

Back in Los Angeles, I lay a single flower down on the spot where I first talked with Doyle. A lot of people look at me as they pass but they don't ask me about the flower or the significance of the spot where I placed it. I think they'd rather believe I hadn't noticed how they were staring. I make my way to the bus station- the first place in LA I stayed at- and pick a ticket-stub up off the ground before climbing aboard a bus. The driver doesn't even ask to see my ticket because of the collar around my throat. Nobody wants to hassle a man of God- especially if he's looking a little beaten up. As best as I can, I retrace my original journey in reverse, heading all the way back to Sinclair. I only pick a couple of pockets to try and get back into the hang of it before stopping in a nondescript town to claim a room at a motel for a reasonable price.

I want to arrive back at my hometown early to mid-morning instead of near dark.

Sinclair is a lot smaller than I remember and all of the colours appear saturated. First I notice the small changes- like how *Dabny's Diner* is now *Caroll's Diner* and *Bob's Hardware* is now *Kreelman's Hardware and Supplies*- but then I notice the stores with boarded doors and windows. It's a sight I'd never have expected to find here.

Not yet ready to see my uncle- that's if he's still breathing- I make my way along Donovan Drive to see if Phil Delano will recognise me like he did my brother all those years gone by. The road is in as bad a state of disrepair as ever; the trailer park has grown, like it's slowly edging its way into the heart of town. There's no trailer with a unicorn painted along its side. Most of them have a sign above the door to let you know who's living there- a true sign that they've admitted defeat and they'll be here a while yet-but I can't find one saying DELANO.

"Shit."

I sigh and light a cigarette, looking out to the motel. Wondering just how many kids have lost their virginity there on prom night only brings an old name to mind... Eleanor Gayle. I smile, take a drag on my cigarette and turn to make my way back into town. A balding man in beige overalls making his way home from work notices the dog-collar I'm wearing and nods on mouthing *hello*. I ask him, "You live here?"

"Sure," he says with a nod, reluctantly stopping to see what it is I'm after.

"You know Phil?"

"Phil?"

"Phil Delano."

"Phil Delano," he says, scratching at the rough stubble underneath his chin. "Never heard of him," the man decides.

"You sure of that?"

"I'm sure."

"Have you lived here long?"

"Not really," he says, "just a couple months- while I'm working out in town. But I haven't heard the name Delano," he says, "and I know everybody staying here."

"I see. Maybe he went and got back with his wife..."

"Maybe," the man shrugs. "That's a good thing, right?"

"Right," I say, walking away. "I'll be seeing you."

"God bless."

I don't head for the Delano family home. I head for the veterinary hospital to see if somebody who featured more prominently in my life will recognise me or not.

67

THE WAITING AREA smells of dog. The benches- used because they sit more people than chairs- are filled with people. Some have a dog at their feet, some hold carriers with a feline inside or a cage housing a bird. Everybody looks to be complimenting everybody else's pet, waiting for something good to be said about their own in return. The receptionist is a dull-looking woman with platinum hair and spectacles that remind me of the large eyes of an owl. She looks up from her computer and to the collar at my throat before taking a silent intake of breath, like her boyfriend works a real dangerous job and I'm here with some bad news.

"Hello," I say, "I'm here to speak with Eleanor."

"She's taking an early lunch in her office."

"Thanks," I nod, "I'll go and find her," I say, turning to walk away. It's been years since I was in here but I'm pretty sure I'll find her office easily enough.

"Is she expecting you?" the receptionist calls after me before reaching for the telephone on her desk either to let her employer know of her visitor or maybe to call security. Back in Los Angeles, I was amazed at how many dental surgeries or veterinary practices had hired security- especially for the nights. It was to stop junkies and other users from targeting the place.

I pass the consultation rooms and the surgery rooms and finally knock at the door of Eleanor's office (long ago, it was her old man's office), pushing the door open just in time to see her placing the receiver of the telephone on her desk back into its cradle. She's sat behind her desk, looking pretty as ever, with a little mayonnaise at the side of her mouth and a baguette with vegetables spilling out of it in front of her. She's aged well. Her tits haven't dropped or she's wearing a decent bra. "Hello," she says, rising to her feet as I close the door shut behind me

180

without taking my eyes off her, "may I help you, Father...?"

"It's Reverend," I smile, taking a step forward that causes her to take a step to the side- like she's prepared for me to start chasing her around her desk with a knife in my hand or something.

"I'm sorry," she says, forcing herself to smile. "Is your pet a patient here?"

I snort. "You really don't recognise me, do you?"

"Should I?" she asks, still looking more than a little concerned.

I smile, hold my left hand up like an old Indian chief so she can see the palm clear enough. "It's been a long while," I tell her, "but your careful hands closed the wound."

She tilts her head to one side. Something flickers behind her eyes and I wonder just what it is she could be thinking.

The door behind me swings open, hitting me in the back. "I'm sorry," the receptionist says to me before looking over my shoulder and at Eleanor. "I see the gentleman found your room," she says. "Would you like me to get you anything... Call anybody?" she asks like I'm too dumb to get onto her little code about calling the law.

"No," Eleanor smiles. "Me and the reverend here are old friends."

"Oh," the receptionist says, clearly a little disappointed about getting all excited over nothing.

Eleanor asks, "Who's manning the front desk?"

"Me. I'll get right back on it," the receptionist replies as she backs out of the office and closes the door behind her. Eleanor moves out from behind her desk and comes walking over to me, taking a real good look at my face with each approaching step.

"You're looking good," I tell her and she responds by slapping me across the face- hard. Then she pulls me close and forces her lips atop of mine, her tongue desperately looking for my own.

68

WE FUCK IN relative silence, neither one of us offering promises or declarations of love to the other and when we're done, we each fix our appearances in that same silence. I look like a respectable man of the cloth whereas she looks like the much loved vet of a small town. Maybe she bakes her own apple pie each weekend?

Eleanor- back in the chair behind her desk as soon as she can manage- takes a wet-wipe from the drawer and rubs it against her hands and between her fingers. I spot the gold band on her wedding finger while she's still cleaning herself up; notice there's no framed picture taken from her wedding day on her desk, no picture of a young child. The thought of asking her to leave her life behind and start another with me comes to mind. It'd be easy enough for her to do if there was no kid involved.

"You married?" I ask, sliding the pack of cigarettes from my pocket with a sigh.

She says, "What?" like I've just pulled her from her own thoughts and she looks to the ring on her finger like she'd forgotten all about it. "Oh," she says. "Yes, I'm married."

"Who's the lucky guy?"

"Alan," she says. "Alan O'Neill." She tosses the wet-wipe into a wastepaper basket, lifts her baguette from the desk but places it back down and looks up at me.

"You want a cigarette?"

"No," she says, "those things will kill you."

"Not always," I shrug, lighting one for myself. "Alan O'Neill? I don't remember him."

"You never knew him," she explains, "I met him at college."

"Oh," I say. "Kids?"

"Not yet."

"I thought not."

"What's that supposed to mean?"

"Nothing," I answer her with a smile. "Have you discussed them?"

She looks at me like she wants to tell me how that's none of my business. "We have," she finally replies. "Not until we're ready."

"When will that be?"

"I don't know," she shrugs, "there's a lot we have to get in order before that day comes. But what about you?" she asks to draw the attention from herself. "Are you an *honest-to-God* reverend?"

"I am," I smirk. "I just finished working out in LA."

"LA? It must be rougher than I imagined. The nose has been broken," she says, "and you look more than a little worn around the edges."

I tell her, "It was an accident. I was playing squash with my neighbour and the ball hit me right in the face. Have you got an ashtray?"

"I don't smoke," she says. I smile, walk around her desk and open a window so I can flick the dead ash of my cigarette out of it. "A reverend," she chuckles.

"Why's that so funny?"

"I don't know," she shrugs, "maybe it's just because you don't act like one? You know- I thought your uncle might have killed you for a while... buried your body in the cellar or something."

"Nah," I say, shaking my head, "some boys run away to join the circus or the army but I went and joined the church." I take a long pull on my cigarette before asking, "He still alive?"

"Yes," she nods, "but he's in pretty bad shape. A carer is with him most days."

"Wow," I sigh. "You're married and my uncle's not as big or as strong as I remember."

"Things change. But what is this," she asks, "the prodigal nephew returning home?"

"Maybe," I shrug. I toss my cigarette out of the window and look at her for a second. "You're still the prettiest girl I have ever seen."

"Thanks."

"I'm serious," I tell her, "you were mine and I blew it. I lost it and I lost you but I never forgot about you... Not truly. I still think we could work- that we were meant to be together. Eleanor," I sigh, "how about you take the band from your finger and me and you give it another try? We can stay here if you want or we can go off and start someplace else."

"It was a long time ago," she says, "and I loved you so much but we had our time and it ended because some things need to... You never lost me- you *left* me."

"Then I was an idiot. But you feel the same, don't you? You want me almost as much as I want you."

"You don't want me," she sighs, "you want an idea of me. You want to recapture something from your past because you think it'll make everything so much better but it can't happen," she explains, "because we're two totally different people to who we were back then. Think like a shark," she says from behind a weak smile, "and remember you have to just keep moving forward."

"I nearly didn't come here... I didn't want you to see me like this. I look in the mirror, I see lines that never used to be there and you look exactly like you did back then whenever I dream about you- which is a lot. You don't look too different in the here and now and I should know," I smile, "because I spotted your ghost at a few places around town. Wearing that pale green hoodie you used to wear when it looked like rain," I laugh, "standing at places where we were going to meet before heading somewhere else."

"Let's hope you turn up," she says without any malice, "because maybe then you will be happy somewhere."

I smile and head for the door. Eleanor says, "Wait," just as I'm pulling it open so I stop and turn to face her. She looks like she has something important to say but isn't too sure how to best go about it. "Are you going back home now?"

"Sure," I nod. "It looks that way."

"How long are you going to be in town for?"

"I don't know," I tell her, "but I'm sure I'll see you around."

She nods, looks at me like what she is about to say pains her but she goes ahead and says it anyway. "Prepare yourself, okay?"

"Okay," I smile. "I hope your husband knows just how lucky

he is.”

69

THE HOUSE HAS been painted recently and you just *know* the gutters are clear. The yard looks nice and homely; even the old mailbox has been touched-up but it still says there is more than one Lee residing at the place. The rusting Ford isn't standing where it was the last time I was here. It must have been moved a long time ago, because I can't see any marks to show where the tyres had rested for so long.

I light a cigarette to steady my nerves and look at the house a little longer. I spotted a couple of familiar faces on the way over here but not one of them seemed to recognise me. I couldn't put a single name to a single face, so maybe I didn't know them after all and that's why they didn't try and talk with me.

The house looks completely different. Could Uncle Nick have married, maybe? Started anew? Become a better man?

It's doubtful. Eleanor would have told me that much, wouldn't she?

Would she have picked up the telephone and spread word of my return? Maybe, if she wanted to get revenge for the way I walked out on her without a single goodbye she could have heard. But I don't think she would have done that. It's too petty.

A car goes by with a couple of high school kids inside, windows down and the volume up. The song they're listening to just happens to be Alice Cooper's *Welcome To My Nightmare* and despite everything, it makes me chuckle a little because it goes with the moment so well. Still smoking, I walk closer to the house- to the front door- and spot the clean mat with WELCOME printed across it right at the door. I didn't think anybody would ever feel welcome here.

I take a final drag on my cigarette and kneel down to check for a key underneath the mat but there isn't one so I flick my cigarette aside and knock at the door. Right away, I notice how hot I'm feeling... how I'm starting to break out in a sweat.

Despite the information Eleanor has given me, I can't help but picture the old man the way I always have… Bigger than me. Stronger. Meaner.

I'm about to turn and walk away with my tail between my legs when the door opens.

70

SHE'LL NO DOUBT be labelled as being Caucasian but I get the feeling there's some African in her genes, maybe only recently or maybe it's decided to come back and haunt her family after skipping a number of generations. She's middle aged and very serious looking. She looks the way a home carer would look in a daytime soap starring Tiffany Lily; tight skin on the face, brown hair kept up in a tidy bun, a crisp white shirt with blue slacks and pumps. "Oh," she says, noticing my tired eyes and uneven, crooked nose to begin with. "Oh," she says again, noticing the collar. Her eyes haven't moved a millimetre but I know how she has taken me in. "May I help you?" she finally asks. I notice the nametag she's wearing at long last. It tells me her name is ROSE.

"Hi," I smile and I'm smiling because I'm wondering if trying to seduce Rose here is worth a shot, "I'm here to see Mr Lee. Are you the carer?"

"Yes," she nods, looking more than a little bit puzzled.

"Reverend Doyle," I say, offering her my hand. "I grew up here... I was a friend of the family."

Rose smiles, releases a sigh and places a hand over her heart. "Oh," she says, "you aren't going to believe this, but I thought maybe you knew something I don't... Like you came here to give him his last rites!"

"Nothing so serious," I smile, hand still waiting for her acceptance. "Mr Lee worked with my old man over at the mill when I was a boy. I just arrived back in town and heard he's taken ill, so I thought I'd come visit."

"How wonderful," she says, stepping aside to let me in without first accepting my offer of a handshake. "I'm sorry to say that Mr Lee doesn't receive too many visitors."

That's understandable.

"That's a shame," I say, entering the home. It smells of strong disinfectant and soap. It looks a lot tidier than it ever did during my time here. "What's wrong with him, exactly?"

"The wrong choices he made have finally caught up with him," she quietly says on closing the door behind her. "How much do you know?"

"Next to nothing," I say, just as quiet. "I heard he's in a bad way and needs a carer most days."

"All days," she sighs. "Would you like to see him now or would you like a coffee first? I can prepare you for what you're about to see if you'd like?"

"Sure," I nod, "I'll take a coffee."

Following her into the kitchen, I glance at his bedroom door and see it's closed. I don't hear him snoring or watching the TV in there, but I wonder if he's awake and trying to figure out just why he somehow recognises my voice. Rose asks, "Do you take sugar or cream?"

I lose my breath and my voice on stepping into the kitchen. It's so clean it sparkles and plenty of sunlight is coming in through the window. It's nothing at all like I remembered it to be. Even the table has gone. No black shirt hangs over the backdoor.

"Yes," I croak, hand diving for my cigarettes and lighter as I clear my throat as best I can. "Black with five sugars, please."

"Five sugars?" Rose laughs. "I'm sorry," she says, "but it's a wonder you have any of your teeth left. That's if you're not wearing dentures," she adds with a smile.

"Men in my line of work have the best dentists," I smile. "We have to have the whitest teeth seeing how we give so many sermons."

Rose laughs and fills two cups with coffee I'm betting she made on arriving here today. "That makes sense," she says, turning to face me with a smile. Her teeth look pretty good. You can see she's trying to decide on the best place to have our coffees, seeing as there's nowhere to sit out here in the kitchen, but I lean back against the nearest worktop and ask her, "Is it okay if I smoke in here?"

Her eyes give the room a quick once-over. "Yes," she says as she puts one of the cups- her own- down on a nearby worktop and takes a step closer to hand me my own, which I graciously accept. "I'll just open the backdoor," she goes on. "I was just making sure there are no oxygen tanks in the room."

"Oxygen tanks?" I ask in horror, flame from my trusty old Zippo already dancing millimetres from the cigarette I've got hanging from my bottom lip.

"Mr Lee needs to use them a couple of times a day," she says, pulling the door open. Fresh air and the scent of flowers drifts in and I wonder if I'm at the wrong address here because of it. Lee is a common name, after all. "His lungs are pretty shot. Smoking," she says, turning to face me.

"You still haven't told me what's wrong with him," I remind her.

"Where to begin?" she asks with a sigh, momentarily looking up at the ceiling. "How long has it been since you last saw him?"

"A good ten years and a few more for good measure," I say and just in case he's been playing it nice and convinced her he's a real nice guy I add, "he was still a hard-drinking man back then. Known for his temper and being real handy with his fists - make no mistake."

"Well," Rose explains, "a lot has happened since then. That lifestyle destroyed him on the inside," she says. "From what I was told, his health was already deteriorating before the cancer got him. They removed it some," she sighs, "but it had already spread. Now we're all just waiting for the end to come and trying to keep him as comfortable as possible until the day finally arrives for him."

I don't ask about the cancer or any of that. I ask, "How long have you been helping him out?"

"Me," she says, "I started last year but the other girl has already been here for two."

"It sure sounds like he's hanging on."

"He is."

I nod, take a deep breath and a sip of my coffee before a quick drag on my cigarette. Rose wants to know, "Are you okay?" It sounds like she truly cares.

"Yeah," I say. "I was a friend of the family... A friend of his nephew, to be precise."

"That's nice," she smiles, unsure of what else there is for her to say. "I was about to walk over to the store," she finally says. "Would you like me to see how he is before you go and speak with him?"

"No," I say, "there's no need. I'll go in and see how he is for myself," I tell her, making my way to the backdoor so I can toss my cigarette outside.

"Before you do," she warns, "don't take it personally if he doesn't recognise you."

I offer her a reassuring smile. "I won't."

"He just mightn't seem as sharp as you remember," she adds with a sigh. "It's the painkillers he's on..."

Taking a deep breath, I place my drink down on the nearest worktop and take confident strides towards his bedroom door.

71

First thing I notice is how the kitchen table is at the end of his bed with a single chair underneath it, like he's some dying Mafia Don insisting he chairs all meetings until he takes his final breath. Or maybe he just has some real fond memories of that table...

The room is kept dark, the blinds closed and the added curtains sealed for extra protection from sunlight that must trouble his eyes. Uncle Nick's asleep or out of it, pillows at his back keeping him in a sitting position as he takes laboured breaths. He's whiter than white and as thin as a single blade of grass. I realise I don't feel any anger or sorrow on seeing him like this. Wanting to wake him, I take the chair from under the table and drag it along the floor so I'll be able to sit at his side. He wakes with a start, eyes rolling around his head for a moment as he tries to make sense of where he is and why. Sitting down, I notice there isn't an oxygen tank in the room and wonder if somebody comes by with one every day and takes it back later that night or something.

His eyes finally fall on me. There's no sense of recognition behind those eyes but you get the feeling he's *trying* to remember me. The tip of his tongue creeps out of his mouth to dab at his dry lips. We just stare at one another in silence until I finally say, "How are you feeling, Mr Lee?"

"You tell me," he mumbles. "Are they expecting me to die today?"

I wait a couple of seconds before giving him an answer. "I'm afraid not," I tell him.

He nods weakly and looks away for a second. His chest rises, shakily, before dropping back down. "I thought today might be the day," he says, "with a priest being sent here."

"Nobody sent me," I say, "I decided to come."

The once powerful Uncle Nick nods again, or he does what

I assume to be a nod. He could have developed a tick of some kind for all I know. "I was a father once," he says. I don't know if he's referring to having children of his own or if he means the years he spent in charge of my brother and me or the times he went out in a black shirt and gave his interpretation of the Bible's teachings on quiet stretches of road so I don't say a word. I wait for him to start up again and he does so soon enough. "My better half," he says.

"Ran out on you because she couldn't handle it."

"I know," he sighs, "I know." He closes his eyes for a long time but no tears are visible when he opens them. I don't even know why I expected him to shed a tear after all this time. "It's probably better to go like she did," he says, "to walk out when the kids are little more than rug-rats. They keep a good picture of you that way, thinking you could do no wrong. They'll forget what you could be like if you die before they're too old. She bailed and left me to become the monster with her sins being forgotten."

I swallow. "Mr Lee," I ask, "would you like to make a confession?"

We both hear the front door open and then close. He looks to me with startled eyes. "What was that?" he asks.

"Just Rose going to the grocery store," I tell him.

"Rose?"

"Your nurse."

"Ah," he says- finally realising who it is exactly we're talking about, "the mongrel. I keep saying I'm fine but nobody will listen... It's just a sprain!"

We sit in silence until I ask him once again, "Would you like to make a confession?"

"Do you remember," he smiles, "when you were young, and we used to go fishing out by the old railway track?"

Panic hits me like a bucket of ice water until I realise we never went fishing, not once. Maybe he thinks I'm his eldest nephew but I don't see how that could be the case what with the changes to my appearance over the years and to the best of my recollection, the two of them never went out fishing together.

I shrug the feeling off, putting it down to nothing other than confusion on his behalf. I tell him, "That wasn't me."

Nick smacks his lips and stares off into the distance. "I popped my cherry out on that old railway track," he says, grinning feebly. "Traded it for Louise Fisher's in the old ticket office. Louise Fisher," he smirks. "Place had already been long disused years before we got there. Place was only good for attracting vermin. We hadn't planned to... We were just drinking and laughing-"

"Mr Lee," I remind him, "would you like to make a confession?"

"My wife," he says, closing his eyes as sleep quickly comes back to collect him once again.

"She left you," I tell him, "just like we all did," but he's already sleeping. I just sit there for a while, looking at him and trying to work out why I feel so disappointed. I mean, what is it I have to feel disappointed about? I run a hand through my hair and get back onto my feet, dragging the chair back under the table. I look at him for a second, take the Zippo from my pocket and put it down on the table before walking out of the room- softly closing the door behind me. I find Rose in the kitchen, making a fresh cup of coffee. "I thought you'd gone."

"Rose," a woman calls out from the back yard and then she's walking into the kitchen and she freezes right there on seeing me.

Mom.

She starts crying and walks at me like a mummy in one of the classic horror movies. "My boy," she says, "my boy."

Rose stands there, frozen to the spot and looking more than a little anxious, as she watches events unfold. Mom pulls me close and struggles to explain what's going on to Rose. "It's been so long," is all she seems able to say.

"Why don't you take the afternoon off, Rose?"

Rose looks at me in a way that makes it easy to see that she wants to accept my offer but doesn't know if she can without being fired. She looks to my mom who nods in approval, almost chokes as she tells Rose she can go. Rose rushes out of the place like her ass is on fire.

Mom takes my face in her hands and says, "Is it really you? I can't believe it's really you."

"It's me," I assure her, "it's me."

72

OUT BACK LOOKS nothing like it used to. Spotless stones in place of unkempt grass and sharp weeds; diamond spaces intentionally placed here and there from which flowers grow. The white plastic table with chairs I'm sitting at must have been put out here so the old man could relax and take in a little sun on a good day. I try not to dwell on the idea of people trying to make Uncle Nick happy.

Mom appears at the back door with two cups of coffee but starts to fall apart on seeing me. She backs out of sight and leaves me with the sounds of her trying to regain her composure. I ignore them. I leave her to suffer alone and light a cigarette instead. Only God can offer true forgiveness. She appears again, red faced and smiling, and makes her way outside and over to the table. For a moment I think she's going to make it but right as she starts lowering the cups her hands begin to shake and she has to quickly place the drinks down and bring her hands back to her face, wiping at the tears. "I'm sorry," she says, "I'm sorry."

"How long have you been back here?" I ask her. I act like I don't give a shit at seeing her upset but I do. I'd rather not have seen her here at all but what do you know- she came back to him. And then there's Eleanor. She gave me the faintest of warnings but as good as left me to come here blind. Walking out on her must have cut her a lot deeper than I could have imagined.

She sits down, places a hand atop of mine and smiles. "I didn't know what happened to you... We were all so worried."

"I ran out to join the church," I reply, deliberately blowing a little smoke towards her. "What'd you run out on your children for?"

She sniffs. "I'm sorry," she says. "My head wasn't in a good place and-"

"*We* weren't in a good place," I interrupt her, "but you still got up and ran."

"I know," she says, "but I'm taking medication now and-"

"Medication," I sneer. "What's that prescribed for- cowardice? Convince yourself it wasn't really you who abandoned your kids with a violent drunk."

"I thought it would be better without me."

I shake my head and drag smoke deep inside my lungs in a bid to push down the urge to jump across the table and strangle the life out of her. "You left us with a man so violent he could kill his own brother."

"No," she says, "no, no, no! That was just a rumour started by fools. Your uncle loved your father. He loved him so much he stepped in and raised you as his own."

"He took a blade to my hand," I tell her. "He tell you about that?"

"Can you imagine the stress he was under? It's not an excuse," she says, "but you have to try and put yourself in his shoes. Out of work and alone with two children. Do you think your father wouldn't have snapped from time to time? Wouldn't have done things he would go and regret for the rest of his days?"

"Don't," I warn her, "compare him to the bastard dying in there."

"You were young when he died," she sighs. "I'll be surprised if you remember much of him. One thing you clearly don't remember is how the Lee men have a temper."

"Right," I smirk. "So when did you come back and why?"

She takes a packet of cigarettes from her jeans. Menthol Lites. I watch her light up and long for cancer to lay claim to the deepest parts of her. "It took me some time but I managed to get my act together," she says. "Managed to stop hating myself and to realise it was worse for me to imagine how much you must hate me than it would be to come back and try to make amends. You and your brother had already gone," she says, "and Nick's health was bad. Not as bad as it is now, but he was a shell of a man."

"He always was," I tell her. "He was a snake in hiding."

She looks down, staring into the darkness of her drink, and

looks back at me with a weak smile. "I thought you people were all about forgiveness?"

"It depends on what day you find me. You see," I smile, "I can be the spirit of an old, vengeful god when pushed."

"Are you threatening me? Your uncle?"

"No," I smirk, "what's the point? You're trapped here in a hell of your own making and as for Nick- look at the sorry son of a bitch. Death would be a mercy to him but there he is, going on. I'm talking about your firstborn son and when we last met-"

"You've seen your brother?"

"Living in a town as dead as this one with a collar around his throat and the wife and daughter. The wife with her secrets and the daughter that just won't listen to him..."

"I don't understand..."

"He had everything," I smile. "He had his own patch of paradise and I took it from him. It looks so perfect to the people passing by but he'll remember, when he's lying there late at night, how I came in and ruined it. Every time he looks to his daughter or wonders what his wife could be doing while he's out at work-"

"Your brother isn't married."

"He is," I laugh, "aren't you listening? Settled down in a nondescript town with a house and-"

"No," she insists, "you aren't listening. Your brother is back *here*," she tells me, "he's been working at the mill for the last eight or so years."

A feeling comes like the world is being snatched away from me and I jump to my feet, desperate to find some solid ground to place them over being lost to the void. "Jesus," I mumble with my face in my hands, "it can't be..."

I think of a good man with a good family in a small town and the wrongs I went and did on him. I think of the black stain that marks him, his wife, his child, the people that came to him for guidance and even his profession, and I can't deny it was me that put it there.

I feel Mom's hand on my shoulder. She's offering words of comfort. She's asking me what it is that has me acting this way but I don't really hear the words. And I try walking away but her hand is still there - she's right beside me - and I tell her, "It's all your fault. Everything that's happened, every wrong I've ever done, it's all on you."

Suddenly the idea of being lost to the void doesn't seem such a bad one. I want to be alone. I want to just burn up among the stars and be forgotten about but she's still there, her hand never leaving my shoulder, and she's saying things that can never repair the damage I've done.

"The fuck away from me," I snap, turning and striking her with the back of my hand. All I can hear is the sound of my own heavy breathing and all I can feel is the delicate tingle dancing along my knuckles. She looks at me, wide-eyed in horror for a second, and then it's clear she has every intention to run.

She's too slow, not as fast as she used to be, and now she has to stay and face her problems. I have one hand at her throat in the blink of an eye, my free hand being drawn back in a clenched fist.

73

THE BLOOD ON my busted knuckles has already congealed. The scratches on the back of my hands are only slightly throbbing now. A rage that possessed my mind and soul so recently feels like it happened not only a lifetime ago but to somebody else. And the knife in my pocket... It's a good knife. You wouldn't use it for skinning a vegetable or anything like that because the blade is only small, an inch or two long, but it's sharp. It could trace the lifeline on your hand without a problem- punch a hole clean through a jugular, even. And I'm calm. I'm as cool as the arctic breeze. Even when I see him come walking out of the mill, laughing and joking with a bunch of his friends, I'm without emotion.

My older brother, John Lee, in the fucking flesh as I live and breathe. There isn't a single doubt in my mind. He carries himself just like he used to, has held onto a lot of the same old mannerisms he'd had back in his youth.

I watch the group cross the street and I take one last drag on my cigarette, drop it to the ground and step down on it before falling in behind them - following them at a safe distance. I can hear the laughter but I can't really make out what they're saying in between... I just know old Johnny looks to be the one taking the lead of this joyous gang of five.

Two of them break away and head over to a car parked across the street and I hope to God that my brother doesn't get to his own car before I have the chance to get him alone. There are waves, more laughs, and one of the group even takes a look at me but it's only a quick glance and then it's all business as usual. I just keep following. I keep following until it's only John and one other and then they split from one another, head in different directions, and I get my big opportunity.

"John," I call out, turning into a gentle jog to catch up with him. He turns and gives me a look, trying and failing to recognise me. "John Lee," I say like I'm asking him a question.

"Yes?" He asks me, "Do I know you?"

"No," I smile before offering him my hand, "I'm afraid not. I'm Reverend Leeson. I'd like to talk with you about your uncle, It's the home care providers," I tell him, "they don't think he's long left so I'd like to find a little out about the man- if it wouldn't be any trouble."

"I don't know," he says as he rubs at the back of his neck, "I'm pretty busy and-"

"Ten minutes over coffee," I insist, "that's all I need."

"Ten minutes," he sighs and then nods. "Okay," he says, "but I've just finished a long shift so would it be okay if we went to a little bar instead?"

"Not at all," I smile, "lead the way, my brother."

74

WE HEAD INTO a place called Leo's and sit down at the bar. I've never been here before. It's a little cramped and dark and the air is too warm and thick. We're the only two people there so the barman heads over to us right away. "Lee," he says with a smile and a nod of his head, "what can I get you?"

"I'll have a bottle of Bud and the reverend here will have..."

"Just a coke, please," I shrug. There's a large mirror on the wall behind the bar, a sign on it reading: PATRONS ARE REMINDED SMOKING IS NOT PERMITTED.

"We only have Pepsi," he says, "is that okay?"

"It's fine," I smile. "Could I have ice and a slice of lime?"

He nods, turns around and sets to preparing our drinks.

"So," my brother turns and says to me, "you really think his time is coming up?"

"When your time comes," I sigh, "it comes," and I start drumming my fingers across the bar but move my hand back down to my side the moment I see him looking to the scratches and bloody knuckles. "I've had quite the morning," I say like it embarrasses me. "I take my frustrations out on the punch bag, then a sweet old girl asks me to encourage her cat out from its hiding place behind the bushes. The cat was not pleased," I laugh.

The barman places our drinks down and asks my brother, "Anything else?"

"No," he says, handing him some money over, "Keep the change."

The barman nods, accepts the payment and walks away to give us some privacy.

John drinks a little beer and savours the cool flavour, looking appreciatively to the chilled bottle for a while like he's trying to sell it in a commercial. "So what is it you'd like to know?" he asks.

"Whatever you'd like to share," I answer. "What kind of man was he? Does he have any family he may not be in contact with that you'd like us to find? Just anything you think I should know."

"The kind of man he was," John smirks. "I'm sorry," he says, "this place is too quiet for my liking. Any requests?" he asks on taking a couple of coins from his back pocket and pointing back to the jukebox against the far wall.

"No," I grin, "I doubt there's any gospel on there."

"Probably not," he laughs and he turns away from me, walks over to the machine and immediately takes to dropping coins into it. I turn and look to my reflection in the mirror, watch as I lift my drink to my lips and drink from it. A song starts playing from the speakers. I don't recognise it. The barman finishes looking over a piece of paper, shakes his head from side to side in disbelief and goes walking out to the back. The door swings open and shut behind him more times than it really should and sometimes I see Doyle is standing back there but at other times he isn't. I turn to look at my dear brother and he's still there, keying his song choices into that fucking jukebox and then I'm on my feet, walking over to him with a hand slipping inside of my pocket.

"This is the second time you've turned your back on me," I hiss into his ear; I have one arm around his throat and he's trying to pry it off but he can't, "and you won't be doing that again."

I bring the knife into his back and he goes as still as stone. I pull back the handle and push the blade deep inside of him three, maybe four times in quick succession and when I let go of him and take a step back he drops straight to the ground and he doesn't move an inch. My breathing is that of a man who's just ran a marathon. I look to the fallen figure at my feet and throw the knife down beside it... Wipe my hands on my trousers on walking away from it. I drink a little more of my Pepsi and head back outside as I'm lighting a smoke. I feel no anger, no sorrow, no relief. I feel nothing.

EPILOGUE

RIGHT AS THE coach driver opens the doors, a squad car appears at the top of the road and comes racing down it with the siren blaring and the lights flashing. I just stand there and watch it as it first nears and then passes. Wherever it's heading to, it isn't here.

The driver asks me without a hint of emotion, "You getting on or what?"

I look behind me- to the man waiting to climb aboard- and see how he's looking at me with disbelief, like my having him wait less than a minute is the biggest insult I can throw at him. I smile at him, nod my head and turn to smile at the driver while climbing aboard. I hold up a ticket I found on an empty seat for him to look through. He nods, turns to look out of the windscreen before the guy behind me has even had a chance to root his own ticket out of his pocket.

The bus is deserted but I make my way to the back anyway and sit down. The driver closes the doors. Doyle asks me where it is we're headed.

"How about America?"

THE END

ACKNOWLEDGEMENTS

To S. Whittaker (master of tech and letters)

and

To Andy Severn (for seeing this done)

and

To the mightily talented Scott Twells
(for great art at the drop of a hat)

Thanks to parents, brothers and sisters, Stevie, G.P. Hewi, Craig Thomas, my hair brother Jean Paul Mills, Tim and numerous people temporarily forgotten.

I fell into something of a habit of listening to the same albums during the writing of this trilogy so it only seems right to name the artists responsible. These are: ...AND YOU WILL KNOW US BY THE TRAIL OF DEAD joseph arthur THE BETA BAND david bowie THE BRIAN JONESTOWN MASSACRE the cooper temple clause THE FALL teenage fanclub JOY DIVISION the olms TESS PARKS rndm TRAMP ATTACK vennart PETE YORN

Give me a year and (some of) these characters will be seen in
THE DEMON JOKE...